We hope you enjoy this book. Please return or renew it by the due date.

You can renew it at www.norfolk.gov.uk/libraries or by using our free library app.

Otherwise you can phone 0344 800 8020 - please have your library card and PIN ready.

You can sign up for email reminders too.

withdrawn from stock

D0726702

NORFOLK COUNTY COUNCIL
LIBRARY AND INFORMATION SERVICE

MURDER
BY
THE SEASIDE

CLASSIC CRIME STORIES FOR SUMMER

Edited by Cecily Gayford

Arthur Conan Doyle · Cyril Hare
John Dickson Carr (Carter Dickson)
G. K. Chesterton · Anthony Berkeley
Michael Innes · Gladys Mitchell
R. Austin Freeman · G. D. H. & M. Cole
Edmund Crispin

P
PROFILE BOOKS

First published in Great Britain in 2022 by
PROFILE BOOKS LTD
29 Cloth Fair
London ECIA 7JQ
www.profilebooks.com

Selection copyright © Profile Books, 2021
See p. 225 for individual stories' copyright information

1 3 5 7 9 10 8 6 4 2

Typeset in Fournier by MacGuru Ltd
Printed and bound in Great Britain by
CPI Group (UK) Ltd, Croydon CRO 4YY

The moral rights of the authors has been asserted.

All rights reserved. Without limiting the rights under copyright
reserved above, no part of this publication may be reproduced,
stored or introduced into a retrieval system, or transmitted, in
any form or by any means (electronic, mechanical, photocopying,
recording or otherwise), without the prior written permission of
both the copyright owner and the publisher of this book.

A CIP catalogue record for this book is available from the British Library.

ISBN 978 1 80081 063 1
eISBN 978 1 80081 065 5

MIX
Paper from
responsible sources
FSC® C171272

Contents

The Boscombe Valley Mystery

Arthur Conan Doyle

We were seated at breakfast one morning, my wife and I, when the maid brought in a telegram. It was from Sherlock Holmes and ran in this way:

'Have you a couple of days to spare? Have just been wired for from the west of England in connection with Boscombe Valley tragedy. Shall be glad if you will come with me. Air and scenery perfect. Leave Paddington by the 11:15.'

'What do you say, dear?' said my wife, looking across at me. 'Will you go?'

'I really don't know what to say. I have a fairly long list at present.'

'Oh, Anstruther would do your work for you. You have been looking a little pale lately. I think that the change would do you good, and you are always so interested in Mr Sherlock Holmes's cases.'

'I should be ungrateful if I were not, seeing what I gained through one of them,' I answered. 'But if I am to go, I must pack at once, for I have only half an hour.'

My experience of camp life in Afghanistan had at least had the effect of making me a prompt and ready traveller. My wants were few and simple, so that in less than the time stated I was in a cab with my valise, rattling away to Paddington Station. Sherlock Holmes was pacing up and down the platform, his tall, gaunt figure made even gaunter and taller by his long grey travelling-cloak and close-fitting cloth cap.

'It is really very good of you to come, Watson,' said he. 'It makes a considerable difference to me, having someone with me on whom I can thoroughly rely. Local aid is always either worthless or else biased. If you will keep the two corner seats I shall get the tickets.'

We had the carriage to ourselves save for an immense litter of papers which Holmes had brought with him. Among these he rummaged and read, with intervals of note-taking and of meditation, until we were past Reading. Then he suddenly rolled them all into a gigantic ball and tossed them up onto the rack.

'Have you heard anything of the case?' he asked.

'Not a word. I have not seen a paper for some days.'

'The London press has not had very full accounts. I have just been looking through all the recent papers in order to master the particulars. It seems, from what I gather, to be one of those simple cases which are so extremely difficult.'

'That sounds a little paradoxical.'

'But it is profoundly true. Singularity is almost invariably a clue. The more featureless and commonplace a crime is, the more difficult it is to bring it home. In this case, however, they have established a very serious case against the son of the murdered man.'

'It is a murder, then?'

'Well, it is conjectured to be so. I shall take nothing for granted until I have the opportunity of looking personally into it. I will explain the state of things to you, as far as I have been able to understand it, in a very few words.

'Boscombe Valley is a country district not very far from Ross, in Herefordshire. The largest landed proprietor in that part is a Mr John Turner, who made his money in Australia and returned some years ago to the old country. One of the farms which he held, that of Hatherley, was let to Mr Charles McCarthy, who was also an ex-Australian. The men had known each other in the colonies, so that it was not unnatural that when they came to settle down they should do so as near each other as possible. Turner was apparently the richer man, so McCarthy became his tenant but still remained, it seems, upon terms of perfect equality, as they were frequently together. McCarthy had one son, a lad of eighteen, and Turner had an only daughter of the same age, but neither of them had wives living. They appear to have avoided the society of the neighbouring English families and to have led retired lives, though both the McCarthys were fond of sport and were frequently seen at the race-meetings of the neighbourhood. McCarthy kept two servants – a man and a girl. Turner had a considerable household, some half-dozen at the least. That is as much as I have been able to gather about the families. Now for the facts.

'On June 3rd, that is, on Monday last, McCarthy left his house at Hatherley about three in the afternoon and walked down to the Boscombe Pool, which is a small lake formed by the spreading out of the stream which runs down the Boscombe Valley. He had been out with his serving-man in the morning at Ross, and he had told the man that he must hurry, as he had an appointment of importance to keep at three. From that appointment he never came back alive.

'From Hatherley Farmhouse to the Boscombe Pool is a quarter of a mile, and two people saw him as he passed over this ground. One was an old woman, whose name is not mentioned, and the other was William Crowder, a game-keeper in the employ of Mr Turner. Both these witnesses depose that Mr McCarthy was walking alone. The game-keeper adds that within a few minutes of his seeing Mr McCarthy pass he had seen his son, Mr James McCarthy, going the same way with a gun under his arm. To the best of his belief, the father was actually in sight at the time, and the son was following him. He thought no more of the matter until he heard in the evening of the tragedy that had occurred.

'The two McCarthys were seen after the time when William Crowder, the game-keeper, lost sight of them. The Boscombe Pool is thickly wooded round, with just a fringe of grass and of reeds round the edge. A girl of fourteen, Patience Moran, who is the daughter of the lodge-keeper of the Boscombe Valley estate, was in one of the woods picking flowers. She states that while she was there she saw, at the border of the wood and close by the lake, Mr McCarthy and his son, and that they appeared to be having a violent quarrel. She heard Mr McCarthy the elder using very strong

4

language to his son, and she saw the latter raise up his hand as if to strike his father. She was so frightened by their violence that she ran away and told her mother when she reached home that she had left the two McCarthys quarrelling near Boscombe Pool, and that she was afraid that they were going to fight. She had hardly said the words when young Mr McCarthy came running up to the lodge to say that he had found his father dead in the wood, and to ask for the help of the lodge-keeper. He was much excited, without either his gun or his hat, and his right hand and sleeve were observed to be stained with fresh blood. On following him they found the dead body stretched out upon the grass beside the pool. The head had been beaten in by repeated blows of some heavy and blunt weapon. The injuries were such as might very well have been inflicted by the butt-end of his son's gun, which was found lying on the grass within a few paces of the body. Under these circumstances the young man was instantly arrested, and a verdict of 'wilful murder' having been returned at the inquest on Tuesday, he was on Wednesday brought before the magistrates at Ross, who have referred the case to the next Assizes. Those are the main facts of the case as they came out before the coroner and the police-court.'

'I could hardly imagine a more damning case,' I remarked. 'If ever circumstantial evidence pointed to a criminal it does so here.'

'Circumstantial evidence is a very tricky thing,' answered Holmes thoughtfully. 'It may seem to point very straight to one thing, but if you shift your own point of view a little, you may find it pointing in an equally uncompromising manner to something entirely different. It must be confessed, however, that the case looks exceedingly grave against the young man, and it is very possible that he is indeed the culprit. There are several people in the neighbourhood, however, and among them Miss Turner, the daughter of the neighbouring land-owner, who believe in his innocence, and who have retained Lestrade, whom you may recollect in connection with the Study in Scarlet, to work out the case in his interest. Lestrade, being rather puzzled, has referred the case to me, and hence it is that two middle-aged gentlemen are flying westward at fifty miles an hour instead of quietly digesting their breakfasts at home.'

'I am afraid,' said I, 'that the facts are so obvious that you will find little credit to be gained out of this case.'

'There is nothing more deceptive than an obvious fact,' he answered, laughing. 'Besides, we may chance to hit upon some other obvious facts which may have been by no means obvious to Mr Lestrade. You know me too well to think that I am boasting when I say that I shall either confirm or destroy his theory by means which he is quite incapable of employing, or even of understanding. To take the first example to hand, I very clearly perceive that in your bedroom the window is upon the right-hand side, and yet I question whether Mr Lestrade would have noted even so self-evident a thing as that.'

'How on earth—'

'My dear fellow, I know you well. I know the military neatness which characterises you. You shave every morning, and in this season you shave by the sunlight; but since your shaving is less and less complete as we get farther back on the left side, until it becomes positively slovenly as we get round the angle of the jaw, it is surely very clear that that side is less illuminated than the other. I could not imagine a man of your habits looking at himself in an equal light and being satisfied with such a result. I only quote this as a trivial example of observation and inference. Therein lies my *métier*, and it is just possible that it may be of some service in the investigation which lies before us. There are one or two minor points which were brought out in the inquest, and which are worth considering.'

'What are they?'

'It appears that his arrest did not take place at once, but after the return to Hatherley Farm. On the inspector of constabulary informing him that he was a prisoner, he remarked that he was not surprised to hear it, and that it was no more than his deserts. This observation of his had the natural effect of removing any traces of doubt which might have remained in the minds of the coroner's jury.'

'It was a confession,' I ejaculated.

'No, for it was followed by a protestation of innocence.'

'Coming on the top of such a damning series of events, it was at least a most suspicious remark.'

'On the contrary,' said Holmes, 'it is the brightest rift which I can at present see in the clouds. However innocent he might be, he could not be such an absolute imbecile as not to see that the circumstances were very black against him. Had he appeared surprised at his own arrest, or feigned indignation at it, I should have looked upon it as highly suspicious, because such surprise or anger would not be natural under the circumstances, and yet might appear to be the best policy to a scheming man. His frank acceptance of the situation marks him as either an innocent man, or else as a man of considerable self-restraint and firmness. As to his remark about his deserts, it was also not unnatural if you consider that he stood beside the dead body of his father, and that there is no doubt that he had that very day so far forgotten his filial duty as to bandy words with him, and even, according to the little girl whose evidence is so important, to raise his hand as if to strike him. The self-reproach and contrition which are displayed in his remark appear to me to be the signs of a healthy mind rather than of a guilty one.'

I shook my head. 'Many men have been hanged on far slighter evidence,' I remarked.

'So they have. And many men have been wrongfully hanged.'

'What is the young man's own account of the matter?'

'It is, I am afraid, not very encouraging to his supporters, though there are one or two points in it which are suggestive. You will find it here, and may read it for yourself.'

He picked out from his bundle a copy of the local Herefordshire paper, and having turned down the sheet he pointed out the paragraph in which the unfortunate young man had given his own statement of what had occurred. I settled myself down in the corner of the carriage and read it very carefully. It ran in this way:

'Mr James McCarthy, the only son of the deceased, was then called and gave evidence as follows: "I had been away from home for three days at Bristol, and had only just returned upon the morning of last Monday, the 3rd. My father was absent from home at the time of my arrival, and I was informed by the maid that he had driven over to Ross with John Cobb, the groom. Shortly after my return I heard the wheels of his trap in the yard, and, looking out of my window, I saw him get out and walk rapidly out of the yard, though I was not aware in which direction he was going. I then took my gun and strolled out in the direction of the Boscombe Pool, with the intention of visiting the rabbit warren which is upon the other side. On my way I saw William Crowder, the game-keeper, as he had stated in his evidence; but he is mistaken in thinking that I was following my father. I had no idea that he was in front of me. When about a hundred yards from the pool I heard a cry of 'Cooee!' which was a usual signal between my father and myself. I then hurried forward, and found him standing by the pool. He appeared to be much surprised at seeing me and asked me rather roughly what I was doing there. A conversation ensued which led to high words and almost to blows, for my father was a man of a very violent temper. Seeing that his passion was becoming ungovernable, I left him and returned towards Hatherley Farm. I had not gone more than 150 yards, however, when I heard a hideous outcry behind me, which caused me to run back again. I found my father expiring upon the ground, with his head terribly injured. I dropped my gun and held him in my arms, but he almost instantly expired. I knelt beside him for some minutes, and then made my way to Mr Turner's lodge-keeper, his house being the nearest, to ask for assistance. I saw no one near my father when I returned, and I have no idea how he came by his injuries. He was not a popular man, being somewhat cold and forbidding in his manners, but he had, as far as I know, no active enemies. I know nothing further of the matter."

The Coroner: "Did your father make any statement to you before he died?"

Witness: "He mumbled a few words, but I could only catch some allusion to a rat."

The Coroner: "What did you understand by that?"

Witness: "It conveyed no meaning to me. I thought that he was delirious."

The Coroner: "What was the point upon which you and your father had this final quarrel?"

Witness: "I should prefer not to answer."

The Coroner: "I am afraid that I must press it."

Witness: "It is really impossible for me to tell you. I can assure you that it has nothing to do with the sad tragedy which followed."

The Coroner: "That is for the court to decide. I need not point out to you that your refusal to answer will prejudice your case considerably in any future proceedings which may arise."

Witness: "I must still refuse."

The Coroner: "I understand that the cry of 'Cooee' was a common signal between you and your father?"

Witness: "It was."

The Coroner: "How was it, then, that he uttered it before he saw you, and before he even knew that you had returned from Bristol?"

Witness (with considerable confusion): "I do not know."

A Juryman: "Did you see nothing which aroused your suspicions when you returned on hearing the cry and found your father fatally injured?"

Witness: "Nothing definite."

The Coroner: "What do you mean?"

Witness: "I was so disturbed and excited as I rushed out into the open, that I could think of nothing except of my father. Yet I have a vague impression that as I ran forward something lay upon the ground to the left of me. It seemed to me to be something grey in colour, a coat of some sort, or a plaid perhaps. When I rose from my father I looked round for it, but it was gone."

"Do you mean that it disappeared before you went for help?"

"Yes, it was gone."

"You cannot say what it was?"

"No, I had a feeling something was there."

"How far from the body?"

"A dozen yards or so."

"And how far from the edge of the wood?"

"About the same."

"Then if it was removed it was while you were within a dozen yards of it?"

"Yes, but with my back towards it."

This concluded the examination of the witness.'

'I see,' said I as I glanced down the column, 'that the coroner in his concluding remarks was rather severe upon young McCarthy. He calls attention, and with reason, to the discrepancy about his father having signalled to him before seeing him, also to his refusal to give details of his conversation with his father, and his singular account of his father's dying words. They are all, as he remarks, very much against the son.'

Holmes laughed softly to himself and stretched himself out upon the cushioned seat. 'Both you and the coroner have been at some pains,' said he, 'to single out the very strongest points in the young man's favour. Don't you see that you alternately give him credit for having too much imagination and too little? Too little, if he could not invent a cause of quarrel which would give him the sympathy of the jury; too much, if he evolved from his own inner consciousness anything so *outré* as a dying reference to a rat, and the incident of the vanishing cloth. No, sir, I shall approach this case from the point of view that what this young man says is true, and we shall see whither that hypothesis will lead us. And now here is my pocket Petrarch, and not another word shall I say of this case until we are on the scene of action. We lunch at Swindon, and I see that we shall be there in twenty minutes.'

It was nearly four o'clock when we at last, after passing through the beautiful Stroud Valley, and over the broad gleaming Severn, found ourselves at the pretty little country-town of Ross. A lean, ferret-like man, furtive and sly-looking, was waiting for us upon the platform. In spite of the light-brown dustcoat and leather-leggings which he wore in deference to his rustic surroundings, I had no difficulty in recognising Lestrade, of Scotland Yard. With him we drove to the Hereford Arms where a room had already been engaged for us.

'I have ordered a carriage,' said Lestrade as we sat over a cup of tea. 'I knew your energetic nature, and that you would not be happy until you had been on the scene of the crime.'

'It was very nice and complimentary of you,' Holmes answered. 'It is entirely a question of barometric pressure.'

Lestrade looked startled. 'I do not quite follow,' he said.

'How is the glass? Twenty-nine, I see. No wind, and not a cloud in the sky. I have a caseful of cigarettes here which need smoking, and the sofa is very much superior to the usual country hotel abomination. I do not think that it is probable that I shall use the carriage tonight.'

Lestrade laughed indulgently. 'You have, no doubt, already formed your conclusions from the newspapers,' he said. 'The case is as plain as a pikestaff, and the more one goes into it the plainer it becomes. Still, of course, one can't refuse a lady, and such a very positive one, too. She has heard of you, and would have your opinion, though I repeatedly told her that there was nothing which you could do which I had not already done. Why, bless my soul! Here is her carriage at the door.'

He had hardly spoken before there rushed into the room one of the most lovely young women that I have ever seen in my life. Her violet eyes shining, her lips parted, a pink flush upon her cheeks, all thought of her natural reserve lost in her overpowering excitement and concern.

'Oh, Mr Sherlock Holmes!' she cried, glancing from one to the other of us, and finally, with a woman's quick intuition, fastening upon my companion, 'I am so glad that you have come. I have driven down to tell you so. I know that James didn't do it. I know it, and I want you to start upon your work knowing it, too. Never let yourself doubt upon that point. We have known each other since we were little children, and I know his faults as no one else does; but he is too tender-hearted to hurt a fly. Such a charge is absurd to anyone who really knows him.'

'I hope we may clear him, Miss Turner,' said Sherlock Holmes. 'You may rely upon my doing all that I can.'

'But you have read the evidence. You have formed some conclusion? Do you not see some loophole, some flaw? Do you not yourself think that he is innocent?'

'I think that it is very probable.'

'There, now!' she cried, throwing back her head and looking defiantly at Lestrade. 'You hear! He gives me hopes.'

Lestrade shrugged his shoulders. 'I am afraid that my colleague has been a little quick in forming his conclusions,' he said.

'But he is right. Oh! I know that he is right. James never did it. And about his quarrel with his father, I am sure that the reason why he would not speak about it to the coroner was because I was concerned in it.'

'In what way?' asked Holmes.

'It is no time for me to hide anything. James and his father had many disagreements about me. Mr McCarthy was very anxious that there should be a marriage between us. James and I have always loved each other as brother and sister; but of course he is young and has seen very little of life yet, and – and – well, he naturally did not wish to do anything like that yet. So there were quarrels, and this, I am sure, was one of them.'

'And your father?' asked Holmes. 'Was he in favour of such a union?'

'No, he was averse to it also. No one but Mr McCarthy was in favour of it.' A quick blush passed over her fresh young face as Holmes shot one of his keen, questioning glances at her.

'Thank you for this information,' said he. 'May I see your father if I call tomorrow?'

'I am afraid the doctor won't allow it.'

'The doctor?'

'Yes, have you not heard? Poor father has never been strong for years back, but this has broken him down completely. He has taken to his bed, and Dr Willows says that he is a wreck and that his nervous system is shattered. Mr McCarthy was the only man alive who had known Dad in the old days in Victoria.'

'Ha! In Victoria! That is important.'

'Yes, at the mines.'

'Quite so; at the gold-mines, where, as I understand, Mr Turner made his money.'

'Yes, certainly.'

'Thank you, Miss Turner. You have been of material assistance to me.'

'You will tell me if you have any news tomorrow. No doubt you will go to the prison to see James. Oh, if you do, Mr Holmes, do tell him that I know him to be innocent.'

'I will, Miss Turner.'

'I must go home now, for Dad is very ill, and he misses me so if I leave him. Goodbye, and God help you in your undertaking.' She hurried from the room as impulsively as she had entered, and we heard the wheels of her carriage rattle off down the street.

'I am ashamed of you, Holmes,' said Lestrade with dignity after a few minutes' silence. 'Why should you raise up hopes which you are bound to disappoint? I am not over-tender of heart, but I call it cruel.'

'I think that I see my way to clearing James McCarthy,' said Holmes. 'Have you an order to see him in prison?'

'Yes, but only for you and me.'

'Then I shall reconsider my resolution about going out. We have still time to take a train to Hereford and see him tonight?'

'Ample.'

'Then let us do so. Watson, I fear that you will find it very slow, but I shall only be away a couple of hours.'

I walked down to the station with them, and then wandered through the streets of the little town, finally returning to the hotel, where I lay upon the sofa and tried to interest myself in a yellow-backed novel. The puny plot of the story was so thin, however, when compared to the deep mystery through which we were groping, and I found my attention wander so continually from the action to the fact, that I at last flung it across the room and gave myself up entirely to a consideration of the events of the day. Supposing that this unhappy young man's story were absolutely true, then what hellish thing, what absolutely unforeseen and extraordinary calamity could have occurred between the time when he parted from his father, and the moment when, drawn back by his screams, he rushed into the glade? It was something terrible and deadly. What could it be? Might not the nature of the injuries reveal something to my medical instincts? I rang the bell and called for the weekly county paper, which contained a verbatim account of the inquest. In the surgeon's deposition it was stated that the posterior third of the left parietal bone and the left half of the occipital bone had been shattered by a heavy blow from a blunt weapon. I marked the spot upon my own head. Clearly such a blow must have been struck from behind. That was to some extent in favour of the accused, as when seen quarrelling he was face to face with his father. Still, it did not go for very much, for the older man might have turned his back before the blow fell. Still, it might be worthwhile to call Holmes's attention to it. Then there was the peculiar dying reference to a rat. What could that mean? It could not be delirium. A man dying from a sudden blow does not commonly become delirious. No, it was more likely to be an attempt to explain how he met his fate. But what could it indicate? I cudgelled my brains to find some possible explanation. And then the incident of the grey cloth seen by young McCarthy. If that were true the murderer must have dropped some part of his dress, presumably his overcoat, in his flight, and must have had the hardihood to return and to carry it away at the instant when the son was kneeling with his back turned not a dozen paces off. What a tissue of mysteries and improbabilities the whole thing was! I did not wonder at Lestrade's opinion, and yet I had so much faith in Sherlock Holmes's insight that I could not lose hope as long as every fresh fact seemed to strengthen his conviction of young McCarthy's innocence.

It was late before Sherlock Holmes returned. He came back alone, for Lestrade was staying in lodgings in the town.

'The glass still keeps very high,' he remarked as he sat down. 'It is of importance that it should not rain before we are able to go over the ground. On the other hand, a man should be at his very best and keenest for such nice work as that, and I did not wish to do it when fagged by a long journey. I have seen young McCarthy.'

'And what did you learn from him?'

'Nothing.'

'Could he throw no light?'

'None at all. I was inclined to think at one time that he knew who had done it and was screening him or her, but I am convinced now that he is as puzzled as everyone else. He is not a very quick-witted youth, though comely to look at and, I should think, sound at heart.'

'I cannot admire his taste,' I remarked, 'if it is indeed a fact that he was averse to a marriage with so charming a young lady as this Miss Turner.'

'Ah, thereby hangs a rather painful tale. This fellow is madly, insanely, in love with her, but some two years ago, when he was only a lad, and before he really knew her, for she had been away five years at a boarding-school, what does the idiot do but get into the clutches of a barmaid in Bristol and marry her at a registry office? No one knows a word of the matter, but you can imagine how maddening it must be to him to be upbraided for not doing what he would give his very eyes to do, but what he knows to be absolutely impossible. It was sheer frenzy of this sort which made him throw his hands up into the air when his father, at their last interview, was goading him on to propose to Miss Turner. On the other hand, he had no means of supporting himself, and his father, who was by all accounts a very hard man, would have thrown him over utterly had he known the truth. It was with his barmaid wife that he had spent the last three days in Bristol, and his father did not know where he was. Mark that point. It is of importance. Good has come out of evil, however, for the barmaid, finding from the papers that he is in serious trouble and likely to be hanged, has thrown him over utterly and has written to him to say that she has a husband already in the Bermuda Dockyard, so that there is really no tie between them. I think that that bit of news has consoled young McCarthy for all that he has suffered.'

'But if he is innocent, who has done it?'

'Ah! Who? I would call your attention very particularly to two points. One is that the murdered man had an appointment with someone at the pool, and that the someone could not have been his son, for his son was away, and he did not know when he would return. The second is that the murdered man was heard to cry "Cooee!" before he knew that his son had returned. Those are the crucial points upon which the case depends. And now let us talk about George Meredith, if you please, and we shall leave all minor matters until tomorrow.'

There was no rain, as Holmes had foretold, and the morning broke bright and cloudless. At nine o'clock Lestrade called for us with the carriage, and we set off for Hatherley Farm and the Boscombe Pool.

'There is serious news this morning,' Lestrade observed. 'It is said that Mr Turner, of the Hall, is so ill that his life is despaired of.'

'An elderly man, I presume?' said Holmes.

'About sixty; but his constitution has been shattered by his life abroad, and he has been in failing health for some time. This business has had a very bad effect upon him. He was an old friend of McCarthy's, and, I may add, a great benefactor to him, for I have learned that he gave him Hatherley Farm rent free.'

'Indeed! That is interesting,' said Holmes.

'Oh, yes! In a hundred other ways he has helped him. Everybody about here speaks of his kindness to him.'

'Really! Does it not strike you as a little singular that this McCarthy, who appears to have had little of his own, and to have been under such obligations to Turner, should still talk of marrying his son to Turner's daughter, who is, presumably, heiress to the estate, and that in such a very cocksure manner, as if it were merely a case of a proposal and all else would follow? It is the more strange, since we know that Turner himself was averse to the idea. The daughter told us as much. Do you not deduce something from that?'

'We have got to the deductions and the inferences,' said Lestrade, winking at me. 'I find it hard enough to tackle facts, Holmes, without flying away after theories and fancies.'

'You are right,' said Holmes demurely; 'you do find it very hard to tackle the facts.'

'Anyhow, I have grasped one fact which you seem to find it difficult to get hold of,' replied Lestrade with some warmth.

'And that is—'

'That McCarthy senior met his death from McCarthy junior and that all theories to the contrary are the merest moonshine.'

'Well, moonshine is a brighter thing than fog,' said Holmes, laughing. 'But I am very much mistaken if this is not Hatherley Farm upon the left.'

'Yes, that is it.' It was a widespread, comfortable-looking building, two-storied, slate-roofed, with great yellow blotches of lichen upon the grey walls. The drawn blinds and the smokeless chimneys, however, gave it a stricken look, as though the weight of this horror still lay heavy upon it. We called at the door, when the maid, at Holmes's request, showed us the boots which her master wore at the time of his death, and also a pair of the son's, though not the pair which he had then had. Having measured these very carefully from seven or eight different points, Holmes desired to be led to the courtyard, from which we all followed the winding track which led to Boscombe Pool.

Sherlock Holmes was transformed when he was hot upon such a scent as this. Men who had only known the quiet thinker and logician of Baker Street would have failed to recognise him. His face flushed and darkened. His brows were drawn into two hard black lines, while his eyes shone out from beneath them with a steely glitter. His face was bent downward, his shoulders bowed, his lips compressed, and the veins stood out like whipcord in his long, sinewy neck. His nostrils seemed to dilate with a purely animal lust for the chase, and his mind was so absolutely concentrated upon the matter before him that a question or remark fell unheeded upon his ears, or, at the most, only provoked a quick, impatient snarl in reply. Swiftly and silently he made his way along the track which ran through the meadows, and so by way of the woods to the Boscombe Pool. It was damp, marshy ground, as is all that district, and there were marks of many feet, both upon the path and amid the short grass which bounded it on either side. Sometimes Holmes would hurry on, sometimes stop dead, and once he made quite a little detour into the meadow. Lestrade and I walked behind him, the detective indifferent and contemptuous, while I watched my friend with the interest which sprang from the conviction that every one of his actions was directed towards a definite end.

The Boscombe Pool, which is a little reed-girt sheet of water some fifty yards across, is situated at the boundary between the Hatherley Farm and the private park of the wealthy Mr Turner. Above the woods which lined it upon the farther side we could see the red, jutting pinnacles which marked the site of the rich landowner's dwelling. On the Hatherley side of the pool the woods grew very thick, and there was a narrow belt of sodden grass twenty paces across between the edge of the trees and the reeds which lined the lake. Lestrade showed us the exact spot at which the body had been found, and, indeed, so moist was the ground, that I could plainly see the traces which had been left by the fall of the stricken man. To Holmes, as I could see by his eager face and peering eyes, very many other things were to be read upon the trampled grass. He ran round, like a dog who is picking up a scent, and then turned upon my companion.

'What did you go into the pool for?' he asked.

'I fished about with a rake. I thought there might be some weapon or other trace. But how on earth—'

'Oh, tut, tut! I have no time! That left foot of yours with its inward twist is all over the place. A mole could trace it, and there it vanishes among the reeds. Oh, how simple it would all have been had I been here before they came like a herd of buffalo and wallowed all over it. Here is where the party with the lodge-keeper came, and they have covered all tracks for six or eight feet round the body. But here are three separate tracks of the same feet.' He drew out a lens and lay down upon his waterproof to have a better view, talking all the time rather to himself than to us. 'These are young McCarthy's feet. Twice he was walking, and once he ran swiftly, so that the soles are deeply marked and the heels hardly visible. That bears out his story. He ran when he saw his father on the ground. Then here are the father's feet as he paced up and down. What is this, then? It is the butt-end of the gun as the son stood listening. And this? Ha, ha! What have we here? Tiptoes! tiptoes! Square, too, quite unusual boots! They come, they go, they come again – of course that was for the cloak. Now where did they come from?' He ran up and down, sometimes losing, sometimes finding the track until we were well within the edge of the wood and under the shadow of a great beech, the largest tree in the neighbourhood. Holmes traced his way to the farther side of this and lay down once more upon his face with a little cry of satisfaction. For a long time he remained there, turning over the leaves and dried sticks, gathering up what seemed to me to be dust into an envelope and examining with his lens not only the ground but even the bark of the tree as far as he could reach. A jagged stone was lying among the moss, and this also he carefully examined and retained. Then he followed a pathway through the wood until he came to the highroad, where all traces were lost.

'It has been a case of considerable interest,' he remarked, returning to his natural manner. 'I fancy that this grey house on the right must be the lodge. I think that I will go in and have a word with Moran, and perhaps write a little note. Having done that, we may drive back to our luncheon. You may walk to the cab, and I shall be with you presently.'

It was about ten minutes before we regained our cab and

drove back into Ross, Holmes still carrying with him the stone which he had picked up in the wood.

'This may interest you, Lestrade,' he remarked, holding it out. 'The murder was done with it.'

'I see no marks.'

'There are none.'

'How do you know, then?'

'The grass was growing under it. It had only lain there a few days. There was no sign of a place whence it had been taken. It corresponds with the injuries. There is no sign of any other weapon.'

'And the murderer?'

'Is a tall man, left-handed, limps with the right leg, wears thick-soled shooting-boots and a grey cloak, smokes Indian cigars, uses a cigar-holder, and carries a blunt penknife in his pocket. There are several other indications, but these may be enough to aid us in our search.'

Lestrade laughed. 'I am afraid that I am still a sceptic,' he said. 'Theories are all very well, but we have to deal with a hard-headed British jury.'

'*Nous verrons*,' answered Holmes calmly. 'You work your own method, and I shall work mine. I shall be busy this afternoon, and shall probably return to London by the evening train.'

'And leave your case unfinished?'

'No, finished.'

'But the mystery?'

'It is solved.'

'Who was the criminal, then?'

'The gentleman I describe.'

'But who is he?'

'Surely it would not be difficult to find out. This is not such a populous neighbourhood.'

Lestrade shrugged his shoulders. 'I am a practical man,' he said, 'and I really cannot undertake to go about the country looking for a left-handed gentleman with a game leg. I should become the laughing-stock of Scotland Yard.'

'All right,' said Holmes quietly. 'I have given you the chance. Here are your lodgings. Goodbye. I shall drop you a line before I leave.'

Having left Lestrade at his rooms, we drove to our hotel, where we found lunch upon the table. Holmes was silent and buried in thought with a pained expression upon his face, as one who finds himself in a perplexing position.

'Look here, Watson,' he said when the cloth was cleared, 'just sit down in this chair and let me preach to you for a little. I don't know quite what to do, and I should value your advice. Light a cigar and let me expound.'

'Pray do so.'

'Well, now, in considering this case there are two points about young McCarthy's narrative which struck us both instantly, although they impressed me in his favour and you against him. One was the fact that his father should, according to his account, cry "Cooee!" before seeing him. The other was his singular dying reference to a rat. He mumbled several words, you understand, but that was all that caught the son's ear. Now from this double point our research must commence, and we will begin it by presuming that what the lad says is absolutely true.'

'What of this "Cooee!" then?'

'Well, obviously it could not have been meant for the son. The son, as far as he knew, was in Bristol. It was mere chance that he was within earshot. The "Cooee!" was meant to attract the attention of whoever it was that he had the appointment with. But "Cooee" is a distinctly Australian cry, and one which is used between Australians. There is a strong presumption that the person whom McCarthy expected to meet him at Boscombe Pool was someone who had been in Australia.'

'What of the rat, then?'

Sherlock Holmes took a folded paper from his pocket and flattened it out on the table. 'This is a map of the Colony of Victoria,' he said. 'I wired to Bristol for it last night.' He put his hand over part of the map. 'What do you read?'

'ARAT,' I read.

'And now?' He raised his hand.

'BALLARAT.'

'Quite so. That was the word the man uttered, and of which his son only caught the last two syllables. He was trying to utter the name of his murderer. So and so, of Ballarat.'

'It is wonderful!' I exclaimed.

'It is obvious. And now, you see, I had narrowed the field down considerably. The possession of a grey garment was a third point which, granting the son's statement to be correct, was a certainty. We have come now out of mere vagueness to the definite conception of an Australian from Ballarat with a grey cloak.'

'Certainly.'

'And one who was at home in the district, for the pool can only be approached by the farm or by the estate, where strangers could hardly wander.'

'Quite so.'

'Then comes our expedition of today. By an examination of the ground I gained the trifling details which I gave to that imbecile Lestrade, as to the personality of the criminal.'

'But how did you gain them?'

'You know my method. It is founded upon the observation of trifles.'

'His height I know that you might roughly judge from the length of his stride. His boots, too, might be told from their traces.'

'Yes, they were peculiar boots.'

'But his lameness?'

'The impression of his right foot was always less distinct than his left. He put less weight upon it. Why? Because he limped – he was lame.'

'But his left-handedness.'

'You were yourself struck by the nature of the injury as recorded by the surgeon at the inquest. The blow was struck from immediately behind, and yet was upon the left side. Now, how can that be unless it were by a left-handed man? He had stood behind that tree during the interview between the father and son. He had even smoked there. I found the ash of a cigar, which my special knowledge of tobacco ashes enables me to pronounce as an Indian cigar. I have, as you know, devoted some attention to this, and written a little monograph on the ashes of 140 different varieties of pipe, cigar and cigarette tobacco. Having found the ash, I then looked round and discovered the stump among the moss where he had tossed it. It was an Indian cigar, of the variety which are rolled in Rotterdam.'

'And the cigar-holder?'

'I could see that the end had not been in his mouth. Therefore he used a holder. The tip had been cut off, not bitten off, but the cut was not a clean one, so I deduced a blunt penknife.'

'Holmes,' I said, 'you have drawn a net round this man from which he cannot escape, and you have saved an innocent human life as truly as if you had cut the cord which was hanging him. I see the direction in which all this points. The culprit is—'

'Mr John Turner,' cried the hotel waiter, opening the door of our sitting room, and ushering in a visitor.

The man who entered was a strange and impressive figure. His slow, limping step and bowed shoulders gave the appearance of decrepitude, and yet his hard, deep-lined, craggy features, and his enormous limbs showed that he was possessed of unusual strength of body and of character. His tangled beard, grizzled hair, and outstanding, drooping eyebrows combined to give an air of dignity and power to his appearance, but his face was of an ashen white, while his lips and the corners of his nostrils were tinged with a shade of blue. It was clear to me at a glance that he was in the grip of some deadly and chronic disease.

'Pray sit down on the sofa,' said Holmes gently. 'You had my note?'

'Yes, the lodge-keeper brought it up. You said that you wished to see me here to avoid scandal.'

'I thought people would talk if I went to the Hall.'

'And why did you wish to see me?' He looked across at my companion with despair in his weary eyes, as though his question was already answered.

'Yes,' said Holmes, answering the look rather than the words. 'It is so. I know all about McCarthy.'

The old man sank his face in his hands. 'God help me!' he cried. 'But I would not have let the young man come to harm. I give you my word that I would have spoken out if it went against him at the Assizes.'

'I am glad to hear you say so,' said Holmes gravely.

'I would have spoken now had it not been for my dear girl. It would break her heart – it will break her heart when she hears that I am arrested.'

'It may not come to that,' said Holmes.

'What?'

'I am no official agent. I understand that it was your daughter who required my presence here, and I am acting in her interests. Young McCarthy must be got off, however.'

'I am a dying man,' said old Turner. 'I have had diabetes for years. My doctor says it is a question whether I shall live a month. Yet I would rather die under my own roof than in a gaol.'

Holmes rose and sat down at the table with his pen in his hand and a bundle of paper before him. 'Just tell us the truth,' he said. 'I shall jot down the facts. You will sign it, and Watson here can witness it. Then I could produce your confession at the last extremity to save young McCarthy. I promise you that I shall not use it unless it is absolutely needed.'

'It's as well,' said the old man; 'it's a question whether I shall live to the Assizes, so it matters little to me, but I should wish to spare Alice the shock. And now I will make the thing clear to you; it has been a long time in the acting, but will not take me long to tell.

'You didn't know this dead man, McCarthy. He was a devil incarnate. I tell you that. God keep you out of the clutches of such a man as he. His grip has been upon me these twenty years, and he has blasted my life. I'll tell you first how I came to be in his power.

'It was in the early 60s at the diggings. I was a young chap then, hot-blooded and reckless, ready to turn my hand at anything; I got among bad companions, took to drink, had no luck with my claim, took to the bush, and in a word became what you would call over here a highway robber. There were six of us, and we had a wild, free life of it, sticking up a station from time to time, or stopping the wagons on the road to the diggings. Black Jack of Ballarat was the name I went under, and our party is still remembered in the colony as the Ballarat Gang.

'One day a gold convoy came down from Ballarat to Melbourne, and we lay in wait for it and attacked it. There were six troopers and six of us, so it was a close thing, but we emptied four of their saddles at the first volley. Three of our boys were killed, however, before we got the swag. I put my pistol to the head of the wagon-driver, who was this very man McCarthy. I wish to the Lord that I had shot him then, but I spared him, though I saw his wicked little eyes fixed on my face, as though to remember every feature. We got away with the gold, became wealthy men, and made our way over to England without being suspected. There I parted from my old pals and determined to settle down to a quiet and respectable life. I bought this estate, which chanced to be in the market, and I set myself to do a little good with my money, to make up for the way in which I had earned it. I

30

married, too, and though my wife died young she left me my dear little Alice. Even when she was just a baby her wee hand seemed to lead me down the right path as nothing else had ever done. In a word, I turned over a new leaf and did my best to make up for the past. All was going well when McCarthy laid his grip upon me.

'I had gone up to town about an investment, and I met him in Regent Street with hardly a coat to his back or a boot to his foot.

'"Here we are, Jack," says he, touching me on the arm; "we'll be as good as a family to you. There's two of us, me and my son, and you can have the keeping of us. If you don't – it's a fine, law-abiding country is England, and there's always a policeman within hail."

'Well, down they came to the West Country, there was no shaking them off, and there they have lived rent free on my best land ever since. There was no rest for me, no peace, no forgetfulness; turn where I would, there was his cunning, grinning face at my elbow. It grew worse as Alice grew up, for he soon saw I was more afraid of her knowing my past than of the police. Whatever he wanted he must have, and whatever it was I gave him without question, land, money, houses, until at last he asked a thing which I could not give. He asked for Alice.

'His son, you see, had grown up, and so had my girl, and as I was known to be in weak health, it seemed a fine stroke to him that his lad should step into the whole property. But there I was firm. I would not have his cursed stock mixed with mine; not that I had any dislike to the lad, but his blood was in him, and that was enough. I stood firm. McCarthy

31

threatened. I braved him to do his worst. We were to meet at the pool midway between our houses to talk it over.

'When I went down there I found him talking with his son, so I smoked a cigar and waited behind a tree until he should be alone. But as I listened to his talk all that was black and bitter in me seemed to come uppermost. He was urging his son to marry my daughter with as little regard for what she might think as if she were a slut from off the streets. It drove me mad to think that I and all that I held most dear should be in the power of such a man as this. Could I not snap the bond? I was already a dying and a desperate man. Though clear of mind and fairly strong of limb, I knew that my own fate was sealed. But my memory and my girl! Both could be saved if I could but silence that foul tongue. I did it, Mr Holmes. I would do it again. Deeply as I have sinned, I have led a life of martyrdom to atone for it. But that my girl should be entangled in the same meshes which held me was more than I could suffer. I struck him down with no more compunction than if he had been some foul and venomous beast. His cry brought back his son; but I had gained the cover of the wood, though I was forced to go back to fetch the cloak which I had dropped in my flight. That is the true story, gentlemen, of all that occurred.'

'Well, it is not for me to judge you,' said Holmes as the old man signed the statement which had been drawn out. 'I pray that we may never be exposed to such a temptation.'

'I pray not, sir. And what do you intend to do?'

'In view of your health, nothing. You are yourself aware that you will soon have to answer for your deed at a higher court than the Assizes. I will keep your confession, and if

McCarthy is condemned I shall be forced to use it. If not, it shall never be seen by mortal eye; and your secret, whether you be alive or dead, shall be safe with us.'

'Farewell, then,' said the old man solemnly. 'Your own deathbeds, when they come, will be the easier for the thought of the peace which you have given to mine.' Tottering and shaking in all his giant frame, he stumbled slowly from the room.

'God help us!' said Holmes after a long silence. 'Why does fate play such tricks with poor, helpless worms? I never hear of such a case as this that I do not think of Baxter's words, and say, "There, but for the grace of God, goes Sherlock Holmes".'

James McCarthy was acquitted at the Assizes on the strength of a number of objections which had been drawn out by Holmes and submitted to the defending counsel. Old Turner lived for seven months after our interview, but he is now dead; and there is every prospect that the son and daughter may come to live happily together in ignorance of the black cloud which rests upon their past.

Weight and See

Cyril Hare

Detective Inspector Mallett of the CID was a very large man. He was not only tall above the average, but also broad in more than just proportion to his height, while his weight was at least proportionate to his breadth. Whether, as his colleagues at New Scotland Yard used to assert, his bulk was due to the enormous meals which he habitually consumed, or whether, as the inspector maintained, the reason for his large appetite was that so big a frame needed more than a normal man's supply for its sustenance, was an open question. What was not open to doubt was Mallett's success in his calling. But if anybody was ever bold enough to suggest that his success might have been even greater but for the handicap of his size he would merely smile sweetly and remark that there had been occasions when on the contrary he had found it a positive advantage. Pressed for further and better particulars, he might, if in an expansive mood, go so far as to say that he could recall at least one case in which he had succeeded where a twelve-stone man would have failed.

This is the story of that case. It is not, strictly speaking, a case of detection at all, since the solution depended ultimately on the chance application of avoirdupois rather than the deliberate application of intelligence. Nonetheless, it was a case which Mallett himself was fond of recollecting, if only because of the way in which that recollection served to salve his conscience whenever thereafter he fell to the temptation of a second helping of suet pudding.

The story begins, so far as the police are concerned, at about seven o'clock on a fine morning in early summer, when a milkman on his round came out of the entrance of Clarence Mansions, SW11, just as a police constable happened to be passing.

'Morning,' said the constable.

'Morning,' said the milkman.

The constable moved on. The milkman stood watching him, two powerful questions conflicting in his breast. On the one hand, it was an article of faith with him that one whose work takes him to other people's houses at a time when most of the world is only beginning to wake up should never poke his nose into other people's business; on the other, he felt just now a craving, new-born but immensely powerful, not to be left out of the adventure which some sixth sense told him was afoot. The constable was almost out of earshot before the issue was decided.

'Oy!' shouted the milkman.

The officer turned round majestically.

'What is it?' he asked.

The milkman jerked his thumb in the direction of the block of flats behind him.

'I don't know,' he said, 'but I think there's something queer up there.'

'Where?'

'Number thirty-two, top floor.'

'How d'you mean, queer?'

'The dog up there is carrying on something awful – barking and scratching at the door.'

'Well, what of it?'

'Oh, nothing, but it's a bit queer, that's all. It's a quiet dog as a rule.'

'They've gone out and left him in, I suppose.'

'Well, if they 'ave, they've left a light on as well.'

The constable looked up at the windows of the top storey.

'There *is* a light on in one of the rooms,' he observed. 'Seems funny, a fine morning like this.' He considered the matter slowly. 'Might as well go up and see, I suppose. They'll be having the neighbours complaining about that dog. I can hear it from here.'

With the milkman in attendance he tramped heavily up the stairs – Clarence Mansions boast no lift – to the top floor. Outside No. 32 stood the pint bottle of milk which had just been left there. He rang the bell. There was no reply, except a renewed outburst of barks from the dog within.

'Are they at home, d'you know?' he asked.

''S far as I know. I 'ad me orders to deliver, same as usual.'

'Who are the people?'

'Wellman, the name is. A little fair chap with a squint. There's just the two of them and the dog.'

'I know him,' said the policeman. 'Seen him about often. Passed the time of day with him. Didn't know he was married, though.'

'She never goes out,' the milkman explained. 'He told me about her once. Used to be a trapeze artist in a circus. 'Ad a fall, and crippled for good. Can't even get in or out of bed by 'erself, so he says.'

'Oh?' said the constable. 'Well, if that's so, perhaps—' He sucked his cheeks and frowned perplexedly. 'All the same, you can't go and break into a place just because the dog's howling and someone's left the light on. I think I'd best go and report this before I do anything.'

The milkman was looking down the staircase.

'Someone coming up,' he announced. 'It's Mr Wellman all right,' he added, as a rather flushed, unshaven face appeared on the landing below.

The constable put on his official manner at once.

'Mr Wellman, sir?' he said. 'There have been complaints of your dog creating a disturbance here this morning. Also I observe that there is a light on in one of your rooms. Would you be good enough to—'

'That's all right, officer,' Wellman interrupted him. 'I was kept out last night. Quite unexpected. Sorry about the dog and all that.'

He fished a latchkey from his pocket, opened the door, and went in, shutting it behind him. The other two, left outside with the milk bottle for company, heard him speak softly to the dog, which immediately became quiet. In the silence they could hear his footsteps down the passage which evidently led away from the front door. They looked at each other blankly. The policeman said 'Well!', the milkman was already preparing to go back to his round, when the steps were heard returning, there was the sound of the door of a room nearby being opened, and then Mr Wellman was out of the flat, his face white, his eyes staring, crying, 'Come here, quick! Something awful has happened!'

'But this,' said Mallett, 'is odd. Very odd indeed.'

He sat in the office of the Divisional Detective Inspector, meditatively turning over a sheaf of reports.

'Odd is the word for it,' the DDI replied. You see, on the one hand there seems no doubt that the lady was alive at nine o'clock—'

'Let me see if I've got the story straight,' said Mallett. 'Mrs Wellman is found dead in her bed at about seven o'clock in the morning by her husband, in the presence, very nearly, of a police officer and another man. She has been killed by a blow on the back of the head from a blunt instrument. The doctor thinks that death occurred about seven to eleven hours previously – say between eight o'clock and midnight the night before. He thinks also – in fact he's pretty sure – that the blow would produce instantaneous death, or at all events instantaneous unconsciousness. There are no signs of forcible entry into the flat, and Mrs Wellman was a cripple, so the possibility of her getting out of bed to let anybody in is out of the question. Am I right so far?'

'Quite correct.'

'In these circumstances the husband quite naturally falls

under suspicion. He is asked to account for his movements overnight, and up to a point he seems quite willing to do so. He says that he put his wife to bed at about a quarter to nine, took the dog out for a short run— What sort of a dog is it, by the way?'

'An Alsatian. It seems to be a good-tempered, intelligent sort of beast.'

'He takes the Alsatian out for a short run, returns it to the flat without going into his wife's room, and then goes out again. That's his story. He says most positively that he never came back to the place until next morning when the constable and the milkman saw him going in. Asked whether he has any witnesses to prove his story, he says that he spoke to the constable on night duty, whom he met just outside Clarence Mansions on his way out, and he further gives the names of two friends whom he met at the Green Dragon public house, half a mile from Clarence Mansions—'

'Seven hundred and fifty yards from Clarence Mansions.'

'I'm much obliged. He met his two pals there at about a quarter-past nine, and stayed there till closing time. He went from the public house with one of them to the nearest tram stop, and took a number thirty-one tram going east, or away from Clarence Mansions. His friend went with him on the tram as far as the next fare stage, where he got off, leaving Wellman on the tram, still going away from home. Is that all clear so far?'

'Quite.'

'Further than that Wellman wouldn't help us. He said he'd spent the rest of the night in a little hotel somewhere down Hackney way. Why he should have done so he didn't explain, and when asked for the name of the place he couldn't give it. He thought it had a red-and-green carpet in the hall, but that's all he could remember about it. The suggestion was, I gather, that he was too drunk to notice things properly when he got to the hotel, and was suffering from a bit of a hangover next morning.'

'He certainly was when I saw him.'

'Things begin to look rather bad for Master Wellman. They look even worse when we find out a few things about him. It seems that he hasn't a job, and hasn't had one for a very long time. He married his wife when she was travelling the country as a trapeze artist in a small circus, in which he was employed as electrician and odd-job man. When a rope broke and she was put out of the circus business for good, her employers paid her a lump sum in compensation. He has been living on that ever since. His accounts show that he has got through it pretty quickly, and it's odds on that she had been wanting to know where it had gone to. It's not very hard to see a motive for getting rid of her.'

'The motive's there all right,' said the Divisional Inspector, 'but—'

'*But*,' Mallett went on. 'Here's where our troubles begin. Wellman is detained for enquiries, and the enquiries show that his story, so far as it goes, is perfectly true. He did meet his pals at the Green Dragon. They and the publican are positive on that point, and they bear out his story in every particular. Therefore if he killed his wife it must have been before a quarter-past nine or after half-past ten, which was approximately the time when he was last seen on the number thirty-one tram. But Mrs Wellman was alive when he left Clarence Mansions, because—'

He pulled out one of the statements before him.

'Statement of Police Constable Denny,' he read. 'At approximately nine o'clock p.m. I was on duty in Imperial Avenue opposite Clarence Mansions when I saw Wellman. He had his dog with him. We had a short conversation. He said, "I've just been giving my dog a run." I said, "It's a nice dog." He said, "I bought it for my wife's protection, but it's too good-natured for a watch-dog." He went into Clarence Mansions and came out again almost at once. He had a small bag in his hand. I said, "Going out again, Mr Wellman?" He said, "Yes. Have you seen my pals about anywhere?" I informed him that I did not know his pals, and he replied, "I expect they're gone on ahead." He then said, "I'm waiting to see if the wife has turned in yet." I looked up at the windows of Clarence Mansions, and there was a light in one of the windows on the top storey – the window to the left of the staircase as you look at it. I have since learned that that is the window of the bedroom of number thirty-two. As I was looking, the light was extinguished. Wellman said to me, "That's all right, I can get along now." We had a bit of a joke about it. He then went away, and I proceeded on my beat. At approximately ten-thirty p.m. I had occasion to pass Clarence Mansions again. There were then no lights visible in the top storey. I did not pass the Mansions again until on my way back from duty at approximately six fifteen a.m. I then observed that the same light was on, but I gave the matter no thought at the time.'

Mallett put down the statement with a sigh.

'What sort of a man is Denny?' he asked.

'Very intelligent and observant,' was the reply. 'One of

the best uniformed men I have. And not too blooming educated, if you follow me.'

'Very well. We have it then on his evidence that Mrs Wellman, or somebody else in the flat, extinguished the light at a little after nine o'clock, and that somebody turned it on again between ten-thirty and six-fifteen. I suppose Mrs Wellman could turn it off and on herself, by the way?'

'Undoubtedly. It was a bedside lamp, and she had the full use of her arms.'

'Therefore,' Mallett went on, 'we are now driven to this – that Wellman killed his wife – if he killed her – after ten-thirty, when he was last seen on the tram, and before midnight, which is the latest time which the doctor thinks reasonably possible. Then comes the blow. To test Wellman's story, for what it is worth, we have made enquiries in Hackney to see if we can find a hotel of the kind that wouldn't mind taking in a gentleman the worse for liquor, with a red-and-green carpet in the hall, and handy to the number thirty-one tram route. And the very first place we try, we not only find that they remember Mr Wellman there but are extremely anxious to see him again. They tell us that he came to their place about half-past eleven – which is the time you would expect if he left the neighbourhood of the Green Dragon by tram an hour before – persuaded whoever it was who was still up at that hour to give him a room, and next morning was seen going out at six o'clock remarking that he was going to get a shave. He never came back—'

'And he never got that shave,' interjected the DDI.

'True enough. And when the hotel people opened his bag

– which Police Constable Denny has identified, incidentally – it contained precisely nothing. So—'

'So we packed him off to the Hackney police to answer a charge of obtaining credit by fraud and asked the Yard to tell us what to do next.'

'In other words, you want me to fix this crime onto somebody who has to all appearances a perfect alibi for it.'

'That's just it,' said the Divisional Inspector in all seriousness. 'If only the blighter had had anything on him that could have been used as a weapon!'

'"On Wellman",' said Mallett, reading from another sheet of the reports, '"were found a pencil, a small piece of cork, a pocket-knife, two shillings silver and sixpence halfpenny bronze." Why,' he continued, 'do we have to go on saying "bronze" when all the rest of the world says "copper", by the way? But the weapon – he could have taken that away in his bag and disposed of it anywhere between here and Hackney easily enough. We shall be lucky if we ever lay our hands on that. The alibi is our trouble. From nine o'clock onwards it seems unbeatable. Therefore he must have killed his wife before nine. But if he did, who was it that turned the light off in her room? I suppose the dog might have done it – knocked the lamp over, or something.'

'There's no trace of the dog having been in the room all night,' said the other. 'His footprints are quite plain on the carpet in the corridor, and I've been over the bedroom carpet carefully without any result. Also, there seems no doubt that the bedroom door was shut next morning. Wellman was heard to unlatch it. Besides, if the dog turned the light off, how did he turn it on again?'

Mallett considered.

'Have you tested the fuses!' he asked.

'Yes, and they are in perfect order. There's no chance of a temporary fault causing the light to go off and on again. And Wellman was waiting for the light to go off when he was talking to Denny.'

'Then,' said Mallett, 'we've got to work on the assumption that someone else got into the flat that night.'

'Without disturbing the dog?'

'A good-natured dog,' Mallett pointed out.

'But there are no signs of any entry whatever. I've looked myself, and some of my best men have been on the job.'

'But I haven't looked yet,' said Mallett.

No. 32 Clarence Mansions was exactly like all the other flats in the block, and indeed in Imperial Avenue, so far as its internal arrangements were concerned. Three very small rooms, looking onto the Avenue, opened out of the corridor which ran from the front door. Three still smaller rooms opened out of another corridor at right angles to the first, and enjoyed a view of the back of the Mansions in the next block. At the junction of the two corridors the gloom of the interior was mitigated by a skylight, the one privilege possessed by the top-storey flats and denied to the rest of the block. The bedroom in which Mrs Wellman had died was the room nearest the entrance.

Mallett did not go into this room until he had first carefully examined the door and the tiny hall immediately inside it.

'There are certainly no marks on the lock,' he said at last.

Then, looking at the floor, he asked, 'What is this powdery stuff down here?'

'Dog biscuit,' was the reply. 'The animal seems to have had his supper here. There's his water-bowl in the corner, too, by the umbrella-stand.'

'But he slept over *there*,' said Mallett, nodding to the farther end of the corridor, where underneath the skylight was a large circular basket, lined with an old rug.

They went into the bedroom. The body had been removed, but otherwise nothing in it had been touched since the discovery of the tragedy. On its dingy walls hung photographs of acrobats, dancers and clowns, and the framed programme of a Command Variety performance – memorials of the trapeze artist's vanished career. The crumpled pillow bore a single shapeless stain of darkened blood. On a bedside table was a cheap electric lamp. Mallett snapped it on and off.

'That doesn't look as if it had been knocked over,' he remarked. 'Did you notice the scratches on the bottom panel of the door, by the way? It seems as though the dog had been trying to get in from the passage.'

He went over to the sash window and subjected it to a prolonged scrutiny.

'No,' he said. 'Definitely, no. Now let's look at the rest of the place.'

He walked down the corridor until he reached the skylight.

'I suppose somebody could have got through here,' he observed.

'But he would have come down right on top of the dog,' the DDI objected.

46

'True. That would have been a bit of a strain for even the quietest animal. Still, there's no harm in looking.'

He kicked aside the sleeping-basket and stood immediately beneath the skylight.

'The light's in my eyes, and I can't see the underside of the frame properly,' he complained, standing on tiptoe and peering upwards. 'Just turn on the electric light, will you? I said, turn on the light,' he repeated in a louder tone.

'It is on,' was the reply, 'but nothing's happened. The bulb must have gone.'

'Has it?' said Mallett, stepping across to the hanging light that swung within a foot of his head. As he did so, the lamp came on.

'Curiouser and curiouser! Switch it off again. Now come and stand where I was.'

They changed places, and Mallett depressed the switch. The light was turned on at once.

'Are you sure you're standing in the same place?'

'Quite sure.'

'Then jump!'

'What?'

'Jump. As high as you can, and come down as hard as you can.'

The inspector sprang into the air, and his heels hit the floor with a crash. At that instant, the light flickered, went out and then came on once more.

'Splendid!' said Mallett. 'Now look between your feet. Do you see anything?'

'There's a little round hole in the floorboard here. That's all.'

'Does the board seem at all loose to you?'

'Yes, it does. Quite a bit. But that's not surprising after what I've done to it.'

'Let me see it.'

Mallett went down on hands and knees and found the hole of which the other had spoken. It was quite small – hardly more than a fault in the wood, but its edges were sharp and clear. It was near to one end of the board. That end was completely unsecured, the other was lightly nailed down. He produced a knife and inserted the blade into the hole. Then, using his knife as a lever, he found that he could pull the board up on its end, as though upon a hinge.

'Look!' he said, and pointed down into the cavity beneath.

On the joist on which the loose end of the board had rested was a small, stiff coiled spring, just large enough to keep that end a fraction above the level of the surrounding floor. But what chiefly attracted the attention of the two men was not on the joist itself but a few inches to one side. It was an ordinary electric bell-push, such as might be seen on any front door in Imperial Avenue.

'Do you recollect what Wellman's job was, when he had a job?' asked Mallett.

'He worked in the circus as odd-job man, and— Good Lord, yes! – electrician.'

'Just so. Now watch!'

He put his finger on the bell-push. The light above their heads went out. He released it, and the light came on again.

'Turn on another light,' said Mallett. 'Any light, I don't care which. In the sitting room, if you like. Now …' He depressed the button once more. 'Does it work?'

'Yes.'

'Of course it does,' he cried triumphantly, rising to his feet and dusting the knees of his trousers. 'The whole thing's too simple for words. The main electric lead of the flat runs under this floor. All Wellman has done is to fit a simple attachment to it, so that when the bell-push is pressed down the circuit is broken and the current turned off. The dog's basket was on this board. That meant that when the dog lay down out went the light in the bedroom – and any other light that happened to be on, only he took care to see that there wasn't any other light on. When the dog begins to get restless in the morning and goes down the passage to see what's the matter – you said he was an intelligent dog, didn't you? – on comes the light again. And anybody in the street outside, seeing the lamp extinguished and lighted again, would be prepared to swear that there was somebody alive in the room to manipulate the lamp. Oh, it really is ingenious!'

'But—' the divisional inspector objected.

'Yes?'

'But the light didn't go off when I was standing there.'

'How much do you weigh?'

'Eleven stone seven.'

'And I'm – well, quite a bit more than that. That's why. You see, there's a fraction of space between the board and the bell-push, and you couldn't quite force the board far enough down to make it work, except when you jumped. I had the advantage over you there,' he concluded modestly.

'But hang it all,' protested the other, 'I may not be a heavy-weight, but I do weigh more than a dog. If I couldn't do the trick, how on earth could he? It doesn't make sense.'

'On Wellman,' said Mallett reflectively, 'were found a pencil, a small piece of cork, a pocket-knife, two shillings silver and sixpence halfpenny bronze. Have you observed that the little hole in the board is directly above the button of the bell-push?'

'Yes. I see now that it is.'

'Very well. If the small piece of cork doesn't fit into that hole, I'll eat your station sergeant's helmet. That's all.'

'So that when the cork is in the hole—'

'When the hole is plugged the end of the cork is resting on the bull-push. It then needs only the weight of the basket, plus the weight of the dog, to depress the spring, which keeps the end of the board up, and the cork automatically works the bell-push. Now we can see what happened. Wellman rigged up this contraption in advance – an easy matter for an experienced electrician. Then, on the evening which he had chosen for the crime, he put his wife to bed, killed her, with the coal hammer most probably – if you search the flat I expect you will find it missing – and shut the door of the bedroom, leaving the bedside lamp alight. He next inserted the cork in the hole of the board and replaced the dog's basket on top. With a couple of dog biscuits in his pocket, he then took the dog out for a run. He kept it out until he saw Police Constable Denny outside the flats. Probably he had informed himself of the times when the officer on duty could be expected to appear there, and made his arrangements accordingly. Having had a word with Denny, he slipped upstairs and let the dog into the flat. But before he came downstairs again he took care to give the dog his biscuits in the hall. It would never have done if the light had been put out before he was out of the building, and he left the dog something to keep him the other end of the passage for a moment or two. He knew that the dog, as soon as he had eaten his supper and had a drink of water, would go and lie down in his basket. I expect he had been trained to do it. Alsatians are teachable animals, they tell me. Down in the street he waited until the dog had put the light out for him, and called Denny's attention to the fact. His alibi established, off he went. But he had to get back next morning to remove that bit of cork. Otherwise the next person who trod on the board might give his secret away. So we find that when he came to the flat the first thing he did was to go down the corridor – before ever he went into the bedroom. That little bit of evidence always puzzled me. Now we know what he was doing. He was a fool not to throw the cork away, of course, but I suppose he thought that nobody would think of looking at that particular place. So far as he knew, nothing could work the lights if the cork wasn't in place. He thought he was safe.

'And,' Mallett concluded, 'he would have been safe too, if there hadn't been that little extra bit of weight put on the board. He couldn't be expected to foresee *me*.'

Which explains, if it does not excuse, the slight but unmistakable touch of condescension with which Inspector Mallett thereafter used to treat his slimmer and slighter brethren.

Error at Daybreak

John Dickson Carr (Carter Dickson)

Under the white light of daybreak, the beach seemed deserted for a full half mile towards the headland. The tide was out, showing a muddy slope at the foot of smooth sand. But it had begun to turn, and flat edges of surf moved snakily back towards the beach.

A narrow lane led down to it, between the high and crooked banks which closed it off from the road. Until you were well out on the sands it was impossible even to see Norman Kane's cottage some distance up towards the right. But one landmark showed in a dark wedge against sand and sea. For several hundred yards out into the water a line of rocks ran in humped formation, curved at the end, in a way that suggested the paw of an animal. It seemed to catch at the incoming tide. Bill Stacey knew it at once for the Lion's Paw, and he set off down the lane towards the beach.

It is to Stacey's credit that he still felt moderately cheerful after having just tramped two miles on an empty stomach, carrying a heavy suitcase. Norman Kane had specified the train he was to take from London, and the wayside station at which it would land him. But Kane had said nothing about a certain lack of transport at that hour of the morning.

The prospect of seeing Marion – Kane's niece and secretary – so cheered him that he forgot the matter. He did not know whether Kane knew he was in love with Marion. Norman Kane had for him the slightly amused tolerance with which Kane would naturally regard an easy-going journalist like Stacey. And Stacey, in turn, had concealed from a hero-worshipping Marion his belief that Norman Kane was an imposing, dignified and strenuous crook.

For in his way Kane was a great man, a power in the City and a company-juggler of skill. And he was genuinely fond of Marion, as he was of all his dependants. With his theatricalism went tireless energy; it was only at Dr Hastings' orders, when he had developed signs of a bad heart, that he had been dragged off for the summer to South Wales.

Heart trouble, Stacey knew, was often the case with these ex-athletes who have run to fat. Kane's worried looks, Marion's worried looks, had disturbed him the last time he saw them. But, as he came out on the beach in the morning light, he felt that nothing ever could happen to Kane.

There was the man himself. Even at a distance he recognised Kane's bulky figure, jauntily wrapped in a dark-red bathrobe with white facings, striding along with a towel over his arm, kicking the sand out of his way with rubber slippers. His bathrobe made a spot of colour against that lonely shore, where the Lion's Paw stretched out into the tide.

And Kane strode out briskly along the Paw. He was not going to bathe. He was going out along the rocks to dive.

'Here!' Stacey said aloud. Swimming, in that sea, with a bad heart? The mutter of the surf was growing as it drove in, and the farther end of the Paw was already awash.

'Ahoy there!' he yelled. 'Kane! Hoy!'

The cry seemed to linger in emptiness across the sands. But it reached Kane, who turned round. He was some fifty yards out on the ridge, but he lifted his towel and waved it.

'Ahoy, my lad!' he bellowed back. 'I didn't expect you so early. Come for a dip! The water's fine. Everything is—'

Then it happened.

Stacey never forgot that big, greyish-haired figure, framed against the sea and the dark crook of the Lion's Paw. He was too far away to catch the expression on Kane's face. But Kane's voice died away in a gulp, a puzzled kind of gulp, and his shoulders drew together. For a moment he stood looking at the beach, swaying a little and pressing his arms as though he were cold. Then he pitched forward on his face like a bag of sand.

It was a second or two before Stacey began to run. As he did so he noticed other figures moving on the beach. From some distance away to the right, in the direction of Kane's cottage, he saw Marion running towards him. There was a gleam on her yellow hair; she wore a bathing suit and a beach robe blown out by the wind. Behind her lumbered Dr Hastings, in a white linen suit.

But Stacey did not wait for them. He knew instinctively that something had happened to Norman Kane, something that was worse than a faint.

Along the top of the Lion's Paw there had been worn a natural sunken path some two feet wide. Picking his way out across this, he found Kane's great bulk wedged into it. Kane's right hand, still clutching the towel, was doubled under him; his left hand lay limply outstretched ahead. Stacey took his pulse, but there was no pulse.

He stood staring down, listening to the slap and swing of the water against the rocks. Heart gone: just like that. At that moment he did not notice the small hole or tear in the back of the dark-red bathrobe, just over the heart. He was too dazed to notice anything more than the fact of death. He hurried back to the beach, where he met Marion and Dr Hastings.

'Steady,' he said, as the girl tried to push past him. 'You'd better go out there, doctor. But I'm afraid he's done for.'

None of them moved. He could not quite estimate the effect of his words on Kane's niece. He realised, too, that he had never before seen Marion without her glasses, which had added a business-like and almost prim touch to her good looks. Over her shoulder towered Dr Hastings, whose wiry, close-cut hair had a Teutonic look, and his expression a Teutonic heaviness.

'Oh!' said the girl. She was looking at him curiously, and she breathed hard. 'Was it – suicide?'

'Suicide?' repeated Stacey, startled. 'No. His heart gave out. Why should you think it was suicide?'

'Oh!' said Marion again. She put her hand on his arm and pressed it. 'I want to see him. No, I'm quite all right. I hope I can move. I can't think very well.'

Dr Hastings, who seemed about to launch a violent

protest, checked himself and pushed past. They went with him to the body, and watched while he made his examination. Then he urged them back towards the beach.

'Look here,' Hastings began heavily. He cleared his throat, and tried again. 'Yes, he's dead right enough; but possibly not for the reason you think. Do you know if Lionel is up yet, Marion?'

So that fellow was at the cottage, thought Stacey. He had never liked the supercilious and aesthetic Mr Lionel Pell. Norman Kane had once courted Lionel's mother, in the days before she had married the late Mr Pell; and this seemed to give Lionel the idea that he had some claim on Kane, particularly with regard to sponging.

'Lionel?' repeated Marion. 'I – I haven't seen him. I got up and went out for an early bathe at the other side of the bay. But I shouldn't think he was up yet. Why?'

'Because,' replied Dr Hastings with his usual directness, 'he'll have to get out his car and drive to the village and get the police. I'm afraid this is murder.'

The surf was driving in now, with deepening thunder. A wave veered against the rocks and flung up a ghostly mane of spray. A cold wind had begun to blow from the south, fluttering Marion's beach robe. She looked at the doctor with rather blind blue eyes, winking as though to keep back tears.

'We had better go up to the house,' Hastings went on heavily, 'and get something to use as a stretcher: he's a weight to move. There are some bad cross-currents out at this distance when the tide rises, and we don't want him washed out to sea before the police get here.'

Then Stacey found his voice.

'The police? Good God, what do you want with the police? His heart—'

'His heart was as sound as yours or mine,' said Hastings.

'So,' said Marion, 'you knew that.'

'I should hope I knew it, my dear girl. I happen to be his doctor. Now keep your chin up and let's face the facts. He's been murdered. What little blood there is doesn't show up well against the dark-red bathrobe; but you probably noticed it. And you may have seen the cut in the back of the bathrobe just over the heart.'

Stacey put his arm round Marion, who had begun to tremble. He spoke with restraint.

'Look here, Doctor. I don't like to suggest that you're out of your mind, but you might come aside and talk nonsense to me instead of talking it to her. Murdered? How could he have been murdered? He was all alone in this path. There wasn't anybody within a hundred yards of him. You must have seen that for yourself.'

'That's true,' put in Marion suddenly. 'I was sitting up at the top of the beach, up under the bank, getting dry; and I saw him go past. That *is* true, Doctor.'

'Yes. It is true. I saw him from the verandah of the cottage,' agreed Hastings.

'Then why all this talk about murder?' asked Stacey. 'Hold on! Are you saying he was shot with a long-range rifle, or something of the sort? It would have to be very long range. His back was towards the sea when he was hit, and there were several miles of empty water behind him.'

'No, I am not saying that.'

'Well?'

'He was killed,' answered Dr Hastings slowly, 'with some kind of steel point like an old-fashioned hatpin. That's what I think, anyhow. I haven't removed it. And I can't swear to the exact nature of the weapon until the post-mortem.'

*

That afternoon, while the grey rain fell, Superintendent Morgan tramped up to the cottage. He had joined the quiet group assembled inside the verandah – Marion, Dr Hastings, Lionel Pell and Bill Stacey sat there. Outside, the sea looked oily and dangerous, as though by its restless movements it were about to burst against the cottage. Superintendent Morgan wore a sou'wester and an oilskin cape; the expression of his face was a contrast to his soft voice.

He glared at Dr Hastings.

'And that's that,' he said. 'I'm suggesting to you, Doctor, that you did this deliberately.'

'You mean,' asked Hastings, examining all sides of the matter, 'that I killed Mr Kane?'

'That is not what I mean. I mean, that you deliberately allowed that body to be washed out to sea. Don't worry. We'll find it. Indeed we will. That was an incoming tide, and it's somewhere along the beach.' The superintendent's light eyes opened. His sing-song voice was more disturbing than violent. 'I say you deliberately let it be carried off so that we shouldn't find out how Mr Kane was killed.'

'Miss Kane and Mr Stacey,' said Hastings shortly, 'will tell you I warned them. I wanted to get a stretcher and move him in time. We were too late, that's all. Why shouldn't I want you to find out how he was killed?'

'Because it's an impossible thing you tell me. The man was alone. No one could have touched him. And yet he was stabbed. There was a way of doing that. If we had found the body we should have known how it was done.'

'Probably you would have,' agreed Hastings.

There was an ominous silence, broken by the flat drizzle of the rain. Bill Stacey, sitting beside Marion, did not look at the superintendent. He found himself more curious about another person, a man who lounged across the verandah near the doorway.

The stranger weighed some seventeen stone and his waterproof made him seem even larger. From under a sodden tweed cap a bland blue eye surveyed the company; and from under a cropped moustache, which might be sandy or grey, there projected a large-bowled pipe, at which he seemed to be sniffing. Stacey had heard the superintendent address him as Colonel March. Colonel March listened, but so far had said nothing.

'Meantime,' said Superintendent Morgan, taking out a notebook, 'there are more queernesses here. I want to hear about them, if you please. Miss Kane!'

Marion glanced up briefly. She had been holding herself in well, Stacey thought, and preserving her blank, 'secretarial' manner.

'We've heard a good deal, hereabouts,' Morgan went on, 'about Mr Kane and his bad heart. You tell us you knew he didn't have a bad heart at all.'

'I guessed it. So did Dr Jones in the village, I think.'

'Then why did he keep on saying he had?' demanded Morgan.

'I – I don't know.'

'Then tell me this, miss. When you first heard this morning that Mr Kane was dead, you asked whether it was suicide. Why did you ask that?'

'I—'

'Truth, miss!'

'I've been worried about him,' answered Marion. 'He's been threatening suicide, if you must know. And he's been acting queerly.'

Lionel Pell intervened. Lionel's way of speaking, which sometimes made him as unintelligible as a gramophone running down, now became almost clear. His long legs were outthrust; and his usual expression of supreme indifference was now replaced by one almost helpful. He sat back, long of nose and jaw, and laid down his pronouncement.

'The word, I believe, is "childish",' he decided. 'The poor old boy – Norman, of course – has been playing with toys. Tell them about the cardboard soldiers, Marion. And the air rifle.'

Marion gave him an almost malevolent look.

'There's nothing very funny or childish about the air rifle. It's a powerful one, hardly a toy at all. You've used it yourself. But I admit I don't understand about the soldiers.'

'You see,' she appealed to Morgan, 'only the night before last my uncle came home with a huge box of cardboard soldiers. He bought them in Cardiff. They were gaudily painted, each of them five or six inches high. In the bottom was a wooden cannon, painted yellow, that fired a hard rubber ball. My uncle went back to his study and unwrapped them, and set them all up on the table.'

At this point, Stacey noticed, the man called Colonel March stirred and glanced across with sudden interest. They all saw it; it brought a new atmosphere of tension. The superintendent looked at her with quick suspicion.

'Did he, Miss Kane? Did he seem to be – er – enjoying himself?'

'No,' she replied quite seriously. 'He looked ill. Once he came out, for no reason at all, and begged my pardon.'

'Miss Kane, do you mean your uncle was insane?'

Dr Hastings interposed. 'Norman Kane,' he said, 'was one of the sanest men I ever met.'

'Now I will tell you something myself,' said Superintendent Morgan. 'He "begged your pardon", you say. You talk of suicide. I have heard of your Mr Kane from my cousin, Morgan David. My cousin tells me that your Mr Kane was not much better than a swindler. My cousin says his companies are crashing, and that he was going to be prosecuted. Is *that* a reason for suicide? I think it is.'

'I know nothing of my uncle's private affairs,' said Marion. And yet it was, Stacey felt, the thing she had been fearing. Marion wore a print frock, and she seemed less like a secretary than a nurse – a nurse at the bedside of a patient who she had determined should not die.

'Is that, I ask you, a reason for suicide?'

'It may be a reason for suicide,' snapped Dr Hastings. 'But it won't explain how a man could run himself through the back at an angle his hand couldn't possibly reach – and in full sight of three witnesses as well.'

'Murder or suicide, it is still impossible!'

'And yet the man is dead.'

'One moment,' said Colonel March.

It was an easy, comfortable voice, and it soothed tempers frayed by rain and fear. His presence was at once authoritative and comfortable, as though he invited them to a discussion rather than an argument; and his amiable eye moved round the group.

'It's not my place to butt in,' he apologised, 'but there are one or two things here that are rather in my line. Do you mind, Superintendent, if I ask a question or two?'

'Glad,' said Morgan fervently. 'This gentleman,' he explained, throwing out his chest, 'is the head of D3 Department at Scotland Yard. He is down here—'

'—on not a very exciting errand,' said Colonel March sadly. 'A matter of a curious thief who steals only green candlesticks, and therefore comes under the head of our special investigation department. Excuse me: Miss Kane, two days before he died your uncle bought a box of cardboard soldiers. Will you get me that box of soldiers now?'

Without a word Marion got up and went into the cottage. Dr Hastings looked up suddenly, as though on the defensive.

'We have also heard,' Colonel March continued presently, 'that he bought an air rifle. I think you used that air rifle, Mr Pell?'

Lionel sat up. With the superintendent he had been friendly and helpful. With Colonel March he had adopted his usual indifference, the air of ease and right with which he (at twenty-three) had called Kane 'Norman' and conferred a favour by accepting loans.

'I *have* used it,' he said. 'It was not my property. Are you under the impression that our late good host was killed by being shot with one of those microscopic pellets out of a toy air rifle? Or, for that matter, by a little rubber ball out of a toy cannon?'

'Where was the air rifle kept?'

You could not shake Lionel's placidity.

'I believe I kept it in my room. Until last night, that is. Then I lent it to Marion. Hadn't you better ask her?'

Marion returned in a few moments, with a large and bright-coloured box, which she handed to Colonel March. She seemed to feel that her name had been mentioned; for she looked quickly between Lionel and Bill Stacey. Colonel March opened the box, sniffing at his pipe.

'And yet,' he said, with a sharpness which made Stacey uneasy, 'the rubber ball is gone. Where, I wonder, is the air rifle now? You borrowed it, Miss Kane?'

'Look here—' interrupted Dr Hastings, with an oddly strained expression. He got up from his chair and sat down again.

'Yes, I borrowed it,' Marion answered. 'Why? Didn't I tell you? I took it out with me when I went to swim this morning, at the other side of the cottage. I shot a few meat tins and things, and then put it down. When I came back to this side of the beach I must have forgotten it.'

She stared at them, her eyes widening.

'I'm afraid it'll be ruined, in all this rain. I'm sorry. But what of it? Is it important?'

'Miss Kane,' said Colonel March, 'do you usually go out for a swim as early in the morning as that?'

'No. Never. Only I was horribly worried about my uncle. I couldn't sleep.'

'You were fond of him?'

'Very fond of him,' said Marion simply. 'He had been very good to me.'

Colonel March's expression seemed to darken and withdraw. It was as expressionless as his ancient cap or his ancient pipe; and he said nothing. But he closed the box of soldiers with great care, and beckoned the superintendent to one side. They had not long to wait for the result.

Late that afternoon a body was washed up on the shore two miles below Barry Island. And Marion Kane was detained for questioning at the police station, as a prelude to formal detention on a charge of murder.

*

Stacey spent one of the worst nights of his life. He told himself that he must keep calm; that he must resist the impulse to telephone wildly for solicitors, invade the police station, and generally make a nuisance of himself. He realised, wryly, that he was not a strong, silent man like Dr Hastings. In difficulties he wanted to do something about them, if only to adopt the dubious course of hitting somebody in the eye.

Things would be all right, he assured himself. Kane's own solicitor was coming from London, and the police were fair. But this very feeling that the police were fair disturbed him worst of all. After a sleepless night at the cottage he dozed off at dawn, and came downstairs at ten o'clock. Lionel Pell was coming up the verandah steps with a newspaper. It was still raining, and so dark that Dr Hastings had lighted the oil lamps in the living room.

'Here's their case,' said Lionel, holding up the newspaper. 'Our superintendent has been talking indiscreetly. It's plastered all over the world.'

'Their case? Their case against——?'

Stacey had to admit that his opinion of Lionel had changed. Lionel had no affectations now; under press of trouble he was only lanky and awkward and human.

'Well, they don't mention her name, of course. She's not officially under arrest. It's very carefully worded. But they appear to have found the air rifle buried in the sand at the top of the beach under the bank. They found it at the exact place where Marion says she was sitting when old Norman fell, and in an almost direct line with the Lion's Paw.'

Against the lamplight from one of the living-room windows appeared Dr Hastings's head. It was only a silhouette with wiry cropped hair, but they saw his knuckles bunch on the window-sill.

'*I* don't know anything about it,' Lionel urged hastily. 'I was in bed and asleep when it happened. But you recall, Bill, that until you came well out on the beach yesterday morning you couldn't see Marion at all. You were in the little lane. Dr Hastings couldn't see her either. He was on the verandah here, and this cottage is set well back behind the line of the bank.

'If Norman were shot in the back, particularly with a weapon like that, he wouldn't feel it the moment he was hit. People don't, they say. He would hear a hail from Bill Stacey, and turn round. Then he would fall forward with the weapon in his heart—'

From the window Hastings uttered a kind of growl.

'The weapon?' he said. 'As a matter of academic interest, will you tell me just what an air rifle has to do with this, anyhow?'

'Oh, come! You won't be able to dodge responsibility like that, Doctor,' said Lionel, who always dodged responsibility.

'Dodge——?'

'Yes. It's your fault. You were the one who suggested that the wound was made by a point and shaft like an old-fashioned hatpin?'

'Well?'

'Those air rifles, you know; they're pretty powerful. Hardly like a toy at all. But sometimes the lead pellets stick in the barrel and clog it. So as a rule the makers give you a very thin, light rod to clean the barrel with. If you cut off about three-quarters of the rod, and sharpen the other end to a needle point, you would have a short missile that could be fired with very damaging force in the ordinary way.'

There was a silence, except for the noise of sea and rain. Stacey walked to the end of the verandah.

'I've heard rot before,' he said, as though making a measured decision. 'But never in my life ... Do you realise that there's no air rifle powerful enough to carry any kind of missile with enough force to kill at a distance of well over fifty yards?'

'Yes, I know,' admitted Lionel. 'But you see the trouble?'

'No, I don't.'

'It's just plausible,' said Lionel. 'I don't believe it. It only worries me.'

'I want my hat,' said Dr Hastings suddenly. 'Where's my hat? This can't go on; I won't have it. I'm going down to the police station to tell them what really happened.'

Outside the cottage there was a rustle of footsteps, stumbling footsteps in the gloom. It was so dark that they could barely see the two persons who came up the steps, but Dr Hastings picked up a lamp inside the window and held it so that the light fell on Colonel March and Marion Kane.

Colonel March was wheezing a little, but as bland as ever. Marion's expression could not be read. There was relief in it, and disillusionment, and even peace; despite the signs of recent emotion, she was smiling.

'I should like a cigarette, please, Bill,' she said. Then she took his arm. 'Thank heavens,' she added, 'for an ordinary decent human being.'

'The superintendent and I,' said Colonel March, 'have come to apologise. Of course, we did what we did entirely with Miss Kane's consent. We have concocted a fiction and kept on the lee side of libel. We have set a trap and heard it snap. We have given you all, I fear, a bad night. But it was the only way we could bring the corpse back to tell his own story ... You had better come up now, Mr Kane.'

It was a very muddy, shamefaced and glowering corpse who walked up the steps behind Superintendent Morgan. Norman Kane, whose heart had stopped beating more than twenty-four hours ago, was now very much alive; and looked as though he wished he weren't.

Norman Kane's grey-haired dignity did not sustain him. He seemed undecided whether or not to hide behind Superintendent Morgan. For a moment he stood opening and shutting his hands. Then he caught sight of Dr Hastings standing in the window, holding up the lamp.

'You traitor,' he roared, and flung himself at the doctor.

*

'He was dead,' insisted Stacey. 'His heart had stopped; I'll swear to that. How did he manage it?'

On a clear, cool morning after the rain, Marion, Stacey and Colonel March stood on the beach looking at a new tide. Colonel March frowned.

'You had better hear the story,' he said. 'Kane was wrong in nearly everything; he was wrong in the way he flared out against Dr Hastings. Hastings is his friend, and only tried to help him when his pig-headed piece of deception would have been discovered in two minutes.

'You will already have guessed the fact which Miss Kane feared: Norman Kane was heading for a bad financial smash. It might not necessarily mean prison, but it would mean ruin and penury. Kane did not like such embarrassments. So he planned to stage a fake death and disappear, with a good sum laid by. Other financiers have been known to do it, you know,' Colonel March added dryly.

Marion shied a pebble at the water and said nothing.

'He was going to "die" and have his body washed out to sea – never to be found,' the colonel went on. 'But he did not want either the stigma of suicide or the prying investigation of a murder. So, with the assistance of Dr Hastings, he arranged to die of heart failure on the Lion's Paw. There had to be an independent witness there to swear to his death: you,

Mr Stacey. You were summoned for that purpose. Hastings had to be there to corroborate you. Then Hastings would shepherd you to the cottage, many hundred yards away, as the tide rose. Kane, a supremely powerful swimmer, could let himself into the water, swim out and round to the headland, and disappear.

'So for a long time he gabbled everywhere about his weak heart. But he would not listen to Hastings, who told him it was very risky. Miss Kane knew that his heart was not weak. Even the village doctor knew it. If Kane, therefore, suddenly dropped dead of a complaint he did not have, there would be a strong suspicion of fraud at the start. It was altogether a foolish plan. Even so it might have gone through if, on the very morning chosen for the "death" Miss Kane had not decided to get up for an early swim.

'She was not accustomed to getting up early, as she told us. Norman Kane and Dr Hastings thought they would have the whole beach to themselves at that hour – except for their special witness: a young man of – er – unsuspicious nature.'

Stacey looked at him gloomily.

'For "unsuspicious",' he said, 'read "imbecile". Very well; but I was in full command of what faculties I have, Colonel. I know when a man is dead. And I tell you his heart had stopped.'

'I beg your pardon,' beamed Colonel March. 'His heart had not stopped. But his pulse had stopped.'

'His pulse?'

'You will recall how he was lying. Flat on his face, with his right hand doubled under him, but his left hand stretched out invitingly. He was also lying wedged in a kind of trough;

70

and you know his enormous weight. To move him and get at his heart would be difficult and awkward. You would never try to do it, with that limp hand stretched out towards you. You would automatically feel the pulse at his wrist. And there was no pulse.'

'But how the dickens can you stop a pulse? It's the same as a heart.'

'You stop it,' said Colonel March, 'by means of a small, hard, rubber ball, such as the little one supplied with the toy cannon in the box of soldiers. It is a good trick, which was exhibited before a group of doctors in London some time ago – and it worked. At the same time it is so simple that I suggest you try it for yourself. Kane, of course, got it from Dr Hastings. The small rubber ball is placed under the armpit. The arm is pressed hard against the side; the flow of blood is cut off; and the man is "dead". Kane lay with his upper arm against his side, but with his lower arm from elbow to wrist extended for your inspection. That is all.

'Even so, the whole plan almost crashed, because Miss Kane appeared on the scene. You, Mr Stacey, had found the body and announced death from heart failure. But Hastings knew that this would never do. Miss Kane strongly suspected that the weak heart was a sham.

'If the body had already been swept out to sea, if she had come on the scene only afterwards, she might have wavered. She might have been uncertain. She might have thought it was suicide, which they tried to conceal from her under a mask of heart failure. But there was the body. If something were not done quickly, she would have insisted on examining it. And it would never do for her to find a living man.'

Marion nodded. She was still shaken from the after-effect of a somewhat bitter hoax, but she thrust out her chin.

'I certainly should have!' she said. 'Only the doctor——'

'Diverted your attention. Exactly. He is an ingenious fellow, Hastings; and no wonder he was upset that morning. He diverted it in the only possible way, with a sudden clap of violence and murder. He drew you hastily back to the beach, so that Kane should not overhear. He shocked you out of your wits, which made it easy for him to put ideas into your mind.

'Remember you never actually *saw* any trace of a wound or a weapon. All you saw was a very minute tear in the back of the dressing-gown, where it had been skagged on a nail.

'That tear (he admits) put the idea into his mind while he was making his "examination". To account for such a very small puncture, and such a complete absence of blood, he had to think of some weapon corresponding to that description; so he postulated something like an old-fashioned hatpin. He could have said it was suicide, of course. But he knew that a man could neither stab himself in the back at that angle, in the presence of witnesses, nor press such a weapon so far into the flesh as to be invisible. Whereas it was just possible that a thin blade might have been projected or fired by a murderer. It was altogether too possible. Dr Hastings had acted wildly and unwisely on the spur of the moment, to prevent the discovery of his friend's hoax. But he must have grown somewhat ill when he saw the case we spun out of a completely harmless air rifle.'

Colonel March smiled apologetically.

'It was a very weak case, of course,' he said, 'but we had

to bring the corpse back. We had to have something – suggestive, but non-committal and non-libellous – to stare at Kane from the Welsh newspapers. It had to be done before he got away to the Continent, or we might never have caught him. The discovery of a drowned body, washed up at Barry, was very helpful; it aided the illusion with which we might snare Kane. The matter was suggested to Miss Kane, who agreed …'

'Agreed?' cried Marion. 'Don't you see I had to know whether … I have looked up to him all my life. I had to know whether he would cut and run just the same if he thought I might be hanged for his murder.'

'Which he did not do,' said Colonel March. 'Mr Norman Kane, I think, has had a refreshing shock which will do him no harm. I should like to have seen him when he crept into town last night; when he found that he was not dead of heart failure and washed out to sea, but that his murdered body has been found and his niece was accused of having killed him. No wonder he burst out at Hastings. But what did he do? He must have realised, Miss Kane, that this charge against you would sooner or later be shown as nonsense; and yet he came back. It was a decent thing to do, as decent as the thing you did yourself. I think it likely that, if he faces his difficulties now, he will save himself as he thought he was saving you.'

The Absence of Mr Glass

G. K. Chesterton

The consulting rooms of Dr Orion Hood, the eminent criminologist and specialist in certain moral disorders, lay along the seafront at Scarborough, in a series of very large and well-lighted French windows, which showed the North Sea like one endless outer wall of blue-green marble. In such a place the sea had something of the monotony of a blue-green dado: for the chambers themselves were ruled throughout by a terrible tidiness not unlike the terrible tidiness of the sea. It must not be supposed that Dr Hood's apartments excluded luxury, or even poetry. These things were there, in their place; but one felt that they were never allowed out of their place. Luxury was there: there stood upon a special table eight or ten boxes of the best cigars; but they were built upon a plan so that the strongest were always nearest the wall and the mildest nearest the window. A tantalus containing three kinds of spirit, all of a liqueur excellence, stood always on this table of luxury; but the fanciful have asserted that the whisky, brandy and rum seemed always to stand at the same level. Poetry was there: the left-hand corner of the room was lined with as complete a set of English classics as the right hand could show of English and foreign physiologists. But if one took a volume of Chaucer or Shelley from that rank, its absence irritated the mind like a gap in a man's front teeth. One could not say the books were never read; probably they were, but there was a sense of their being chained to their places, like the Bibles in the old churches. Dr Hood treated his private bookshelf as if it were a public library. And if this strict scientific intangibility steeped even the shelves laden with lyrics and ballads and the tables laden with drink and tobacco, it goes without saying that yet more of such heathen holiness protected the other shelves that held the specialist's library, and the other tables that sustained the frail and even fairylike instruments of chemistry or mechanics.

Dr Hood paced the length of his string of apartments, bounded – as the boys' geographies say – on the east by the North Sea and on the west by the serried ranks of his sociological and criminologist library. He was clad in an artist's velvet, but with none of an artist's negligence; his hair was heavily shot with grey, but growing thick and healthy; his face was lean, but sanguine and expectant. Everything about him and his room indicated something at once rigid and restless, like that great northern sea by which (on pure principles of hygiene) he had built his home.

Fate, being in a funny mood, pushed the door open and introduced into those long, strict, sea-flanked apartments one who was perhaps the most startling opposite of them and their master. In answer to a curt but civil summons, the door opened inwards and there shambled into the room a shapeless little figure, which seemed to find its own hat and umbrella as unmanageable as a mass of luggage. The umbrella was a black and prosaic bundle long past repair; the hat was a broad-curved black hat, clerical but not common in England; the man was the very embodiment of all that is homely and helpless.

The doctor regarded the newcomer with a restrained astonishment, not unlike that he would have shown if some huge but obviously harmless sea-beast had crawled into his room. The newcomer regarded the doctor with that beaming but breathless geniality which characterises a corpulent charwoman who has just managed to stuff herself into an omnibus. It is a rich confusion of social self-congratulation and bodily disarray. His hat tumbled to the carpet, his heavy umbrella slipped between his knees with a thud; he reached after the one and ducked after the other, but with an unimpaired smile on his round face spoke simultaneously as follows:

'My name is Brown. Pray excuse me. I've come about that business of the MacNabs. I have heard you often help people out of such troubles. Pray excuse me if I am wrong.'

By this time he had sprawlingly recovered the hat, and made an odd little bobbing bow over it, as if setting everything quite right.

'I hardly understand you,' replied the scientist, with a cold intensity of manner. 'I fear you have mistaken the chambers. I am Dr Hood, and my work is almost entirely literary and educational. It is true that I have sometimes been consulted by the police in cases of peculiar difficulty and importance, but—'

'Oh, this is of the greatest importance,' broke in the little man called Brown. 'Why, her mother won't let them get engaged.' And he leaned back in his chair in radiant rationality.

The brows of Dr Hood were drawn down darkly, but the eyes under them were bright with something that might be anger or might be amusement. 'And still,' he said, 'I do not quite understand.'

'You see, they want to get married,' said the man with the clerical hat. 'Maggie MacNab and young Todhunter want to get married. Now, what can be more important than that?'

The great Orion Hood's scientific triumphs had deprived him of many things – some said of his health, others of his God; but they had not wholly despoiled him of his sense of the absurd. At the last plea of the ingenuous priest a chuckle broke out of him from inside, and he threw himself into an armchair in an ironical attitude of the consulting physician.

'Mr Brown,' he said gravely, 'it is quite fourteen and a half years since I was personally asked to test a personal problem: then it was the case of an attempt to poison the French President at a Lord Mayor's Banquet. It is now, I understand, a question of whether some friend of yours called Maggie is a suitable fiancée for some friend of hers called Todhunter. Well, Mr Brown, I am a sportsman. I will take it on. I will give the MacNab family my best advice, as good as I gave the French Republic and the King of England – no, better: fourteen years better. I have nothing else to do this afternoon. Tell me your story.'

78

The little clergyman called Brown thanked him with unquestionable warmth, but still with a queer kind of simplicity. It was rather as if he were thanking a stranger in a smoking room for some trouble in passing the matches, than as if he were (as he was) practically thanking the curator of Kew Gardens for coming with him into a field to find a four-leaved clover. With scarcely a semicolon after his hearty thanks, the little man began his recital:

'I told you my name was Brown; well, that's the fact, and I'm the priest of the little Catholic Church I dare say you've seen beyond those straggly streets, where the town ends towards the north. In the last and straggliest of those streets which runs along the sea like a sea wall there is a very honest but rather sharp-tempered member of my flock, a widow called MacNab. She has one daughter, and she lets lodgings, and between her and the daughter, and between her and the lodgers – well, I dare say there is a great deal to be said on both sides. At present she has only one lodger, the young man called Todhunter; but he has given more trouble than all the rest, for he wants to marry the young woman of the house.'

'And the young woman of the house,' asked Dr Hood, with huge and silent amusement, 'what does she want?'

'Why, she wants to marry him,' cried Father Brown, sitting up eagerly. 'That is just the awful complication.'

'It is indeed a hideous enigma,' said Dr Hood.

'This young James Todhunter,' continued the cleric, 'is a very decent man so far as I know; but then nobody knows very much. He is a bright, brownish little fellow, agile like a monkey, clean-shaven like an actor, and obliging like a born courtier. He seems to have quite a pocketful of money, but nobody knows what his trade is. Mrs MacNab, therefore (being of a pessimistic turn), is quite sure it is something dreadful, and probably connected with dynamite. The dynamite must be of a shy and noiseless sort, for the poor fellow only shuts himself up for several hours of the day and studies something behind a locked door. He declares his privacy is temporary and justified, and promises to explain before the wedding. That is all that anyone knows for certain, but Mrs MacNab will tell you a great deal more than even she is certain of. You know how the tales grow like grass on such a patch of ignorance as that. There are tales of two voices heard talking in the room; though, when the door is opened, Todhunter is always found alone. There are tales of a mysterious tall man in a silk hat, who once came out of the sea mists and apparently out of the sea, stepping softly across the sandy fields and through the small back garden at twilight, till he was heard talking to the lodger at his open window. The colloquy seemed to end in a quarrel. Todhunter dashed down his window with violence, and the man in the high hat melted into the sea fog again. This story is told by the family with the fiercest mystification; but I really think Mrs MacNab prefers her own original tale: that the Other Man (or whatever it is) crawls out every night from the big box in the corner, which is kept locked all day. You see, therefore, how this sealed door of Todhunter's is treated as the gate of all the fancies and monstrosities of the "Thousand and One Nights". And yet there is the little fellow in his respectable black jacket, as punctual and innocent as a parlour clock. He pays his rent to the tick; he is practically a teetotaller; he is tirelessly kind with the younger children, and can keep them amused for a day on end; and, last and most urgent of all, he has made himself equally popular with the eldest daughter, who is ready to go to church with him tomorrow.'

A man warmly concerned with any large theories has always a relish for applying them to any triviality. The great specialist having condescended to the priest's simplicity, condescended expansively. He settled himself with comfort in his armchair and began to talk in the tone of a somewhat absent-minded lecturer:

'Even in a minute instance, it is best to look first to the main tendencies of Nature. A particular flower may not be dead in early winter, but the flowers are dying; a particular pebble may never be wetted with the tide, but the tide is coming in. To the scientific eye all human history is a series of collective movements, destructions or migrations, like the massacre of flies in winter or the return of birds in spring. Now the root fact in all history is Race. Race produces religion; Race produces legal and ethical wars. There is no stronger case than that of the wild, unworldly and perishing stock which we commonly call the Celts, of whom your friends the MacNabs are specimens. Small, swarthy and of this dreamy and drifting blood, they accept easily the superstitious explanation of any incidents, just as they still accept (you will excuse me for saying) that superstitious explanation of all incidents which you and your Church represent. It is not remarkable that such people, with the sea moaning behind them and the Church (excuse me again) droning in front of them, should put fantastic features into what are probably plain events. You, with your small parochial responsibilities, see only this particular Mrs MacNab, terrified with this particular tale of two voices and a tall man out of the sea. But the man with the scientific imagination sees, as it were, the whole clans of MacNab scattered over the whole world, in its ultimate average as uniform as a tribe of birds. He sees thousands of Mrs MacNabs, in thousands of houses, dropping their little drop of morbidity in the teacups of their friends; he sees—'

Before the scientist could conclude his sentence, another and more impatient summons sounded from without; someone with swishing skirts was marshalled hurriedly down the corridor, and the door opened on a young girl, decently dressed but disordered and red-hot with haste. She had sea-blown blonde hair, and would have been entirely beautiful if her cheekbones had not been, in the Scotch manner, a little high in relief as well as in colour. Her apology was almost as abrupt as a command.

'I'm sorry to interrupt you, sir,' she said, 'but I had to follow Father Brown at once; it's nothing less than life or death.'

Father Brown began to get to his feet in some disorder. 'Why, what has happened, Maggie?' he said.

'James has been murdered, for all I can make out,' answered the girl, still breathing hard from her rush. 'That man Glass has been with him again; I heard them talking through the door quite plain. Two separate voices: for James speaks low, with a burr, and the other voice was high and quavery.'

'That man Glass?' repeated the priest in some perplexity.

'I know his name is Glass,' answered the girl, in great impatience. 'I heard it through the door. They were quarrelling

— about money, I think — for I heard James say again and again, "That's right, Mr Glass", or "No, Mr Glass", and then, "Two or three, Mr Glass". But we're talking too much; you must come at once, and there may be time yet.'

'But time for what?' asked Dr Hood, who had been studying the young lady with marked interest. 'What is there about Mr Glass and his money troubles that should impel such urgency?'

'I tried to break down the door and couldn't,' answered the girl shortly, 'Then I ran to the backyard, and managed to climb on to the window-sill that looks into the room. It was all dim, and seemed to be empty, but I swear I saw James lying huddled up in a corner, as if he were drugged or strangled.'

'This is very serious,' said Father Brown, gathering his errant hat and umbrella and standing up; 'in point of fact I was just putting your case before this gentleman, and his view—'

'Has been largely altered,' said the scientist gravely. 'I do not think this young lady is so Celtic as I had supposed. As I have nothing else to do, I will put on my hat and stroll down town with you.'

In a few minutes all three were approaching the dreary tail of the MacNabs' street: the girl with the stern and breathless stride of the mountaineer, the criminologist with a lounging grace (which was not without a certain leopard-like swiftness), and the priest at an energetic trot entirely devoid of distinction. The aspect of this edge of the town was not entirely without justification for the doctor's hints about desolate moods and environments. The scattered houses stood farther and farther apart in a broken string along the seashore; the afternoon was closing with a premature and partly lurid twilight; the sea was of an inky purple and murmuring ominously. In the scrappy back garden of the MacNabs which ran down towards the sand, two black, barren-looking trees stood up like demon hands held up in astonishment, and as Mrs MacNab ran down the street to meet them with lean hands similarly spread, and her fierce face in shadow, she was a little like a demon herself. The doctor and the priest made scant reply to her shrill reiterations of her daughter's story, with more disturbing details of her own, to the divided vows of vengeance against Mr Glass for murdering, and against Mr Todhunter for being murdered, or against the latter for having dared to want to marry her daughter, and for not having lived to do it. They passed through the narrow passage in the front of the house until they came to the lodger's door at the back, and there Dr Hood, with the trick of an old detective, put his shoulder sharply to the panel and burst in the door.

It opened on a scene of silent catastrophe. No one seeing it, even for a flash, could doubt that the room had been the theatre of some thrilling collision between two, or perhaps more, persons. Playing cards lay littered across the table or fluttered about the floor as if a game had been interrupted. Two wine glasses stood ready for wine on a side table, but a third lay smashed in a star of crystal upon the carpet. A few feet from it lay what looked like a long knife or short sword, straight, but with an ornamental and pictured handle; its dull blade just caught a grey glint from the dreary window behind, which showed the black trees against the leaden level of the sea. Towards the opposite corner of the room was rolled a gentleman's silk top hat, as if it had just been knocked off his head; so much so, indeed, that one almost looked to see it still rolling. And in the corner behind it, thrown like a sack of potatoes, but corded like a railway trunk, lay Mr James Todhunter, with a scarf across his mouth, and six or seven ropes knotted round his elbows and ankles. His brown eyes were alive and shifted alertly.

Dr Orion Hood paused for one instant on the doormat and drank in the whole scene of voiceless violence. Then he stepped swiftly across the carpet, picked up the tall silk hat, and gravely put it upon the head of the yet pinioned Todhunter. It was so much too large for him that it almost slipped down onto his shoulders.

'Mr Glass's hat,' said the doctor, returning with it and peering into the inside with a pocket lens. 'How to explain the absence of Mr Glass and the presence of Mr Glass's hat? For Mr Glass is not a careless man with his clothes. That hat is of a stylish shape and systematically brushed and burnished, though not very new. An old dandy, I should think.'

'But, good heavens!' called out Miss MacNab, 'aren't you going to untie the man first?'

'I say "old" with intention, though not with certainty,' continued the expositor; 'my reason for it might seem a little far-fetched. The hair of human beings falls out in very varying degrees, but almost always falls out slightly, and with the lens I should see the tiny hairs in a hat recently worn. It has none, which leads me to guess that Mr Glass is bald. Now when this is taken with the high-pitched and querulous voice which Miss MacNab described so vividly (patience, my dear lady, patience), when we take the hairless head together with the tone common in senile anger, I should think we may deduce some advance in years. Nevertheless, he was probably vigorous, and he was almost certainly tall. I might rely in some degree on the story of his previous appearance at the window, as a tall man in a silk hat, but I think I have more exact indication. This wine glass has been smashed all over the place, but one of its splinters lies on the high bracket beside the mantelpiece. No such fragment could have fallen there if the vessel had been smashed in the hand of a comparatively short man like Mr Todhunter.'

'By the way,' said Father Brown, 'might it not be as well to untie Mr Todhunter?'

'Our lesson from the drinking vessels does not end here,' proceeded the specialist. 'I may say at once that it is possible that the man Glass was bald or nervous through dissipation rather than age. Mr Todhunter, as has been remarked, is a quiet, thrifty gentleman, essentially an abstainer. These cards and wine cups are no part of his normal habit; they have been produced for a particular companion. But, as it happens, we may go farther. Mr Todhunter may or may not possess this wine service, but there is no appearance of his possessing any wine. What, then, were these vessels to contain? I would at once suggest some brandy or whisky, perhaps of a luxurious sort, from a flask in the pocket of Mr Glass. We have thus something like a picture of the man, or at least of the type: tall, elderly, fashionable, but somewhat frayed, certainly fond of play and strong waters, perhaps rather too fond of them. Mr Glass is a gentleman not unknown on the fringes of society.'

'Look here,' cried the young woman, 'if you don't let me pass to untie him I'll run outside and scream for the police.'

'I should not advise you, Miss MacNab,' said Dr Hood gravely, 'to be in any hurry to fetch the police. Father Brown, I seriously ask you to compose your flock, for their sakes, not for mine. Well, we have seen something of the figure and quality of Mr Glass; what are the chief facts known of Mr Todhunter? They are substantially three: that he is economical, that he is more or less wealthy, and that he has a secret. Now, surely it is obvious that there are the three chief marks of the kind of man who is blackmailed. And surely it is equally obvious that the faded finery, the profligate habits, and the shrill irritation of Mr Glass are the unmistakable marks of the kind of man who blackmails him. We have the two typical figures of a tragedy of hush money: on the one hand, the respectable man with a mystery; on the other, the West End vulture with a scent for a mystery. These two men have met here today and have quarrelled, using blows and a bare weapon.'

'Are you going to take those ropes off?' asked the girl stubbornly.

Dr Hood replaced the silk hat carefully on the side table, and went across to the captive. He studied him intently, even moving him a little and half-turning him round by the shoulders, but he only answered:

'No; I think these ropes will do very well till your friends the police bring the handcuffs.'

Father Brown, who had been looking dully at the carpet, lifted his round face and said: 'What do you mean?'

The man of science had picked up the peculiar dagger-sword from the carpet and was examining it intently as he answered:

'Because you find Mr Todhunter tied up,' he said, 'you all jump to the conclusion that Mr Glass had tied him up; and then, I suppose, escaped. There are four objections to this: First, why should a gentleman so dressy as our friend Glass leave his hat behind him, if he left of his own free will? Second,' he continued, moving towards the window, 'this is the only exit, and it is locked on the inside. Third, this blade here has a tiny touch of blood at the point, but there is no wound on Mr Todhunter. Mr Glass took that wound away with him, dead or alive. Add to all this primary probability. It is much more likely that the blackmailed person would try to kill his incubus, rather than that the blackmailer would try to kill the goose that lays his golden egg. There, I think, we have a pretty complete story.'

'But the ropes?' enquired the priest, whose eyes had remained open with a rather vacant admiration.

'Ah, the ropes,' said the expert with a singular intonation. 'Miss MacNab very much wanted to know why I did not set Mr Todhunter free from his ropes. Well, I will tell her. I did not do it because Mr Todhunter can set himself free from them at any minute he chooses.'

'What?' cried the audience on quite different notes of astonishment.

'I have looked at all the knots on Mr Todhunter,' reiterated Hood quietly. 'I happen to know something about knots; they are quite a branch of criminal science. Every one of those knots he has made himself and could loosen himself;

not one of them would have been made by an enemy really trying to pinion him. The whole of this affair of the ropes is a clever fake, to make us think him the victim of the struggle instead of the wretched Glass, whose corpse may be hidden in the garden or stuffed up the chimney.'

There was a rather depressed silence; the room was darkening, the sea-blighted boughs of the garden trees looked leaner and blacker than ever, yet they seemed to have come nearer to the window. One could almost fancy they were sea monsters like krakens or cuttlefish, writhing polypi who had crawled up from the sea to see the end of this tragedy, even as he, the villain and victim of it, the terrible man in the tall hat, had once crawled up from the sea. For the whole air was dense with the morbidity of blackmail, which is the most morbid of human things, because it is a crime concealing a crime; a black plaster on a blacker wound.

The face of the little Catholic priest, which was commonly complacent and even comic, had suddenly become knotted with a curious frown. It was not the blank curiosity of his first innocence. It was rather that creative curiosity which comes when a man has the beginnings of an idea. 'Say it again, please,' he said in a simple, bothered manner; 'do you mean that Todhunter can tie himself up all alone and untie himself all alone?'

'That is what I mean,' said the doctor.

'Jerusalem!' ejaculated Brown suddenly, 'I wonder if it could possibly be that!'

He scuttled across the room rather like a rabbit, and peered with quite a new impulsiveness into the partially covered face of the captive. Then he turned his own rather

89

fatuous face to the company. 'Yes, that's it!' he cried in a certain excitement. 'Can't you see it in the man's face? Why, look at his eyes!'

Both the professor and the girl followed the direction of his glance. And though the broad black scarf completely masked the lower half of Todhunter's visage, they did grow conscious of something struggling and intense about the upper part of it.

'His eyes do look queer,' cried the young woman, strongly moved. 'You brutes; I believe it's hurting him!'

'Not that, I think,' said Dr Hood; 'the eyes have certainly a singular expression. But I should interpret those transverse wrinkles as expressing rather such slight psychological abnormality—'

'Oh, bosh!' cried Father Brown: 'can't you see he's laughing?'

'Laughing!' repeated the doctor, with a start; 'but what on earth can he be laughing at?'

'Well,' replied the Reverend Brown apologetically, 'not to put too fine a point on it, I think he is laughing at you. And indeed, I'm a little inclined to laugh at myself, now I know about it.'

'Now you know about what?' asked Hood, in some exasperation.

'Now I know,' replied the priest, 'the profession of Mr Todhunter.'

He shuffled about the room, looking at one object after another with what seemed to be a vacant stare, and then invariably bursting into an equally vacant laugh, a highly irritating process for those who had to watch it. He laughed very much over the hat, still more uproariously over the broken glass, but the blood on the sword point sent him into mortal convulsions of amusement. Then he turned to the fuming specialist.

'Dr Hood,' he cried enthusiastically, 'you are a great poet! You have called an uncreated being out of the void. How much more godlike that is than if you had only ferreted out the mere facts! Indeed, the mere facts are rather commonplace and comic by comparison.'

'I have no notion what you are talking about,' said Dr Hood rather haughtily; 'my facts are all inevitable, though necessarily incomplete. A place may be permitted to intuition, perhaps (or poetry if you prefer the term), but only because the corresponding details cannot as yet be ascertained. In the absence of Mr Glass—'

'That's it, that's it,' said the little priest, nodding quite eagerly, 'that's the first idea to get fixed; the absence of Mr Glass. He is so extremely absent. I suppose,' he added reflectively, 'that there was never anybody so absent as Mr Glass.'

'Do you mean he is absent from the town?' demanded the doctor.

'I mean he is absent from everywhere,' answered Father Brown; 'he is absent from the Nature of Things, so to speak.'

'Do you seriously mean,' said the specialist with a smile, 'that there is no such person?'

The priest made a sign of assent. 'It does seem a pity,' he said.

Orion Hood broke into a contemptuous laugh. 'Well,' he said, 'before we go on to the hundred and one other evidences, let us take the first proof we found; the first fact we

91

fell over when we fell into this room. If there is no Mr Glass, whose hat is this?'

'It is Mr Todhunter's,' replied Father Brown.

'But it doesn't fit him,' cried Hood impatiently. 'He couldn't possibly wear it!'

Father Brown shook his head with ineffable mildness. 'I never said he could wear it,' he answered. 'I said it was his hat. Or, if you insist on a shade of difference, a hat that is his.'

'And what is the shade of difference?' asked the criminologist with a slight sneer.

'My good sir,' cried the mild little man, with his first movement akin to impatience, 'if you will walk down the street to the nearest hatter's shop, you will see that there is, in common speech, a difference between a man's hat and the hats that are his.'

'But a hatter,' protested Hood, 'can get money out of his stock of new hats. What could Todhunter get out of this one old hat?'

'Rabbits,' replied Father Brown promptly.

'What?' cried Dr Hood.

'Rabbits, ribbons, sweetmeats, goldfish, rolls of coloured paper,' said the reverend gentleman with rapidity. 'Didn't you see it all when you found out the faked ropes? It's just the same with the sword. Mr Todhunter hasn't got a scratch on him, as you say; but he's got a scratch in him, if you follow me.'

'Do you mean inside Mr Todhunter's clothes?' enquired Mrs MacNab sternly.

'I do not mean inside Mr Todhunter's clothes,' said Father Brown. 'I mean inside Mr Todhunter.'

'Well, what in the name of Bedlam do you mean?'

'Mr Todhunter,' explained Father Brown placidly, 'is learning to be a professional conjurer, as well as juggler, ventriloquist and expert in the rope trick. The conjuring explains the hat. It is without traces of hair, not because it is worn by the prematurely bald Mr Glass, but because it has never been worn by anybody. The juggling explains the three glasses, which Todhunter was teaching himself to throw up and catch in rotation. But, being only at the stage of practice, he smashed one glass against the ceiling. And the juggling also explains the sword, which it was Mr Todhunter's professional pride and duty to swallow. But, again, being at the stage of practice, he very slightly grazed the inside of his throat with the weapon. Hence he has a wound inside him, which I am sure (from the expression on his face) is not a serious one. He was also practising the trick of a release from ropes, like the Davenport Brothers, and he was just about to free himself when we all burst into the room. The cards, of course, are for card tricks, and they are scattered on the floor because he had just been practising one of those dodges of sending them flying through the air. He merely kept his trade secret, because he had to keep his tricks secret, like any other conjurer. But the mere fact of an idler in a top hat having once looked in at his back window, and been driven away by him with great indignation, was enough to set us all on a wrong track of romance, and make us imagine his whole life overshadowed by the silk-hatted spectre of Mr Glass.'

'But what about the two voices?' asked Maggie, staring.

'Have you never heard a ventriloquist?' asked Father Brown. 'Don't you know they speak first in their natural voice, and then answer themselves in just that shrill, squeaky, unnatural voice that you heard?'

There was a long silence, and Dr Hood regarded the little man who had spoken with a dark and attentive smile. 'You are certainly a very ingenious person,' he said; 'it could not have been done better in a book. But there is just one part of Mr Glass you have not succeeded in explaining away, and that is his name. Miss MacNab distinctly heard him so addressed by Mr Todhunter.'

The Rev. Mr Brown broke into a rather childish giggle. 'Well, that,' he said, 'that's the silliest part of the whole silly story. When our juggling friend here threw up the three glasses in turn, he counted them aloud as he caught them, and also commented aloud when he failed to catch them. What he really said was: "One, two and three – missed a glass one, two – missed a glass." And so on.'

There was a second of stillness in the room, and then everyone with one accord burst out laughing. As they did so the figure in the corner complacently uncoiled all the ropes and let them fall with a flourish. Then, advancing into the middle of the room with a bow, he produced from his pocket a big bill printed in blue and red, which announced that ZALADIN, the World's Greatest Conjurer, Contortionist, Ventriloquist and Human Kangaroo would be ready with an entirely new series of Tricks at the Empire Pavilion, Scarborough, on Monday next at eight o'clock precisely.

Razor Edge

Anthony Berkeley

The bathing around Penhampton is notoriously dangerous. In consequence the mortuary of the local police force
is larger than usual, for swimmers are obstinate people, and
though the wide sandy reaches of Penhampton beach itself
are well guarded, the few miles of rocky coast in either direction, with its many coves and little bays, are impossible to
supervise.

It was therefore no surprise to the borough police when
a body was reported among the rocks of Sandymouth cove
on a sunny July afternoon. The usual routine was set in
motion, the body collected and brought to the mortuary, and
the temporary assurance obtained from the police surgeon
that death was due to drowning. A careful description of the
body was taken, but any enquiries as to its ownership were
made unnecessary by a visitor to the police station.

It was five o'clock, and Superintendent Thomas, having

signed all the documents awaiting his attention, was thinking of going home when his sergeant clerk told him that a woman was in the charge-room reporting that her husband had gone bathing in Sandymouth cove that morning and had not returned.

'I'd better see her,' sighed the superintendent, thinking of the garden he wanted to water, and put his hat back again on the rack.

The woman had given her name as Mrs Hutton. Particulars of her husband's name, profession and address had already been taken, and these were laid discreetly on the superintendent's table as the sergeant showed her into the room. The woman was fair and a somewhat faded thirty-five though still with traces of a youthful prettiness, and she was in a state of some agitation.

'Sit down, Mrs Hutton,' soothed the superintendent. 'Now – you're worried about your husband?'

The woman nodded, choked, and said: 'Yes. He went out bathing this morning. I was to join him later. His clothes were on the beach, but – oh, I'm sure – I'm sure—'

'Now, now,' said the superintendent mechanically, and asked for further particulars.

These took some minutes to obtain, but finally reduced themselves to the following facts. Mr Edward Hutton, described as a financier with an office in the City and a home in Streatham, was staying with his wife at Ocean View Boarding House in the little village of Penmouth, about five miles west of Penhampton. He had left his lodgings at about half-past ten that morning, telling his wife that he was going to bathe, probably in company with a certain Mr Barton, who was camping alone on top of the cliffs of Sandymouth Bay: a Mr Michael Somerville Barton, whom Mrs Hutton vaguely believed to be a writer and novelist, from London. Mrs Hutton was to join the two men at about noon; but when she arrived, though their wraps were still on the beach, no sign of either man was to be seen. She had called and searched, and then returned to her boarding house. In the afternoon, being now thoroughly worried, she decided after discussing the matter with her landlady to come into Penhampton and report to the police.

The superintendent nodded. 'And the description of your husband, madam?'

Mrs Hutton leaned back in her chair and closed her eyes. 'My husband is five foot seven inches tall, not very broad, thinnish arms and legs, thirty-four inches chest measurement, rather long hands and feet, medium brown hair, clean-shaven, grey-green eyes, and rather pale complexion; he has an old appendicitis scar, and – oh, yes, and there is a big mole on his left shoulder blade.'

The superintendent could not restrain his admiration. 'Upon my word, Mrs Hutton, you reeled that off a treat. Very different from some of them I assure you.'

'I – I was thinking it out in the bus,' said the woman faintly. 'I knew you'd want a description.'

'Yes. Well—' Surreptitiously the superintendent studied the description of the body now in the mortuary. It tallied in every particular. He became aware that the sergeant was speaking.

'Excuse me, sir, could the lady give us a good description of Barton, the other gentleman?'

'No, I'm afraid—' Mrs Hutton hesitated. 'I've only met him once, for a few minutes. I can't really tell you – he had a long moustache.'

'We can get a description from Mr Turner, sir,' interposed the sergeant tactfully. 'It's in one of his fields that Mr Barton was camping.'

The superintendent nodded and then, with much sympathetic throat-clearing, proceeded to the distasteful task of warning Mrs Hutton to prepare for a shock. He was very much afraid that in the mortuary now – if Mrs Hutton would come along for a moment   …

He sighed again as the woman gave every sign of imminent hysterics.

'He's here already? Must I see him? Must I? Won't – won't the description do?'

It took five minutes to get her into the mortuary.

But once there she regained her calm. A curious dead-alive look came into her own face as she stared down into the other dead one from which the superintendent had gently withdrawn the sheet.

'Yes,' she whispered, tonelessly. 'That's my husband. That's – Eddie.'

Then she fainted.

*

Roger Sheringham was staying a weekend with Major Drake, the chief constable of Penhampton. They were old friends, with a common interest in crime.

So far, however, Roger had been disappointed. The

Penhampton police was a very small force and his host, though a bachelor, had been unable to enliven the previous evening by tales of grisly murder in his district, for the good reason that his district had never had a murder. When therefore the major announced that on their way to the golf course he had to call in at Police Headquarters to take formal view of some poor stiff who had got himself drowned the day before, Roger pricked up his ears.

'And by the way,' added the major, 'you may be able to help us a bit. Ever hear of a chap called Barton in your line? Writes books and things, y'know. Michael Somerville Barton. Hey?'

'Yes, I've heard of him, but I don't know him. A bit too Bloomsbury for me, I fancy. Why?'

'Because he's probably dead.'

'What, murdered?'

'No, *not* murdered. Just plain drowned.'

'People have been murdered by drowning before now,' Roger pointed out mildly.

'Well, this one wasn't. Good lord, Sheringham, you amateur detectives! A corpse in every cupboard, and every death a murder, eh? Haven't you ever heard of such a thing as an accident?'

'Very well: how did Michael Somerville Barton meet his accidental death by drowning?'

'Oh, went bathing with another fellow yesterday morning. Lonely bit of coast. Neither of them seen again. Damn fools, they will do it, in spite of our notices. It's the other fellow's body I've got to look at. Very humdrum and ordinary, I'm afraid. Hurry up with that coffee.'

'I've finished.'

'Then come on. Got your clubs?'

'They're in the hall.'

'Not they. They'll have been put in the cupboard under the stairs by this time. A place for everything and everything in its place in this house, my boy.'

With pride the major threw open the cupboard door and extracted his own clubs. Roger's were not there. They were finally found standing in a corner of the hall.

'Come, Drake,' Roger said. 'The house isn't so bad as you make out.'

It was only a few minutes' ride to the police station, where on the steps a plainclothesman greeted them respectfully. The chief constable introduced him as Detective Inspector Clarke, in charge of the small CID section. Roger was childishly pleased to note the look of interest on the inspector's face as they shook hands.

The little party went through to the superintendent's office, where they picked up the large and comfortable man and also the police doctor who happened to be in the building; and after the details of the case had been recited on one side and duly absorbed on the other, a move was made to the mortuary.

'Pasty-faced beggar, eh?' was the chief constable's comment, as they stood in a circle round the slab that bore the dead man.

'He's certainly no advertisement for you,' Roger agreed. '"Penhampton for Bonnie Sunshine", eh? Perhaps you haven't had any bonnie sunshine lately?'

'Hot and sunny all the week,' retorted the major. 'He can't have been here long, that's all.'

'The Huttons arrived on the twelfth, sir,' put in the inspector. 'That's about ten days ago.'

'Then this fellow was no sunbather,' Roger commented. 'Or else he wore a panama. Queer how some men actually prefer hats.'

'Come now, Sheringham,' said the chief constable impatiently. 'Don't begin making difficulties. His forehead's got a bit of brown to it.'

'And the skin on his nose looks as if it might have begun to peel at any moment. What more could Penhampton want?'

'Well, Superintendent, if that's all—'

The major's intention of escaping was however temporarily frustrated, for at that moment the sergeant clerk arrived to say that he was wanted on the telephone, by Scotland Yard.

'Scotland Yard, eh?' repeated the major, obviously gratified. 'What on earth do they want? Some dam' red tape, no doubt.' He went, followed by the superintendent who obviously took no chances.

Roger felt it up to him to make conversation. 'You've made your examination, doctor? Death due to drowning all right.'

'Oh, yes,' the doctor nodded. 'No doubt about that. His lungs were chock-full of water.'

'Why, did you notice anything, Mr Sheringham?' the inspector asked eagerly.

'Afraid not, this time,' Roger laughed. 'Except that Mr Hutton wasn't so spruce as he might have been.'

'How do you make that out?'

'He hadn't shaved yesterday morning.'

'Sorry, but he had,' corrected the doctor with a smile.

'That cut's fresh, at the side of his mouth. If it had been made the day before, it would have been half healed.'

'And yet there's plenty of stubble on his chin. Queer.'

'Oh, if you're interested in queer details,' said the doctor, 'have a look at the scratches on his back.'

'What scratches?'

The doctor signed to the inspector, and the two of them turned the corpse over. Roger saw that the skin on the back was badly lacerated, from the shoulders to the small of the back, while the elbows were almost raw.

'Barnacles,' explained the doctor shortly. 'There are barnacles on the rocks here?'

'Covered with them. And it was among the rocks that the body was found. Still—'

Roger nodded. 'I see what you mean. If the body was washing about, why did it only get lacerated in that particular area? It is queer. Very queer.'

'But there's a simple explanation, after all,' the doctor smiled. 'The man who found him pulled him by the legs to where he could pick him up more easily. That's all.'

'No, sir,' put in the inspector respectfully. 'The body was wedged under a big rock at the side of a pool. Trewin, the farm hand who happened to find him when he went down for a pail of sea water, says he picked him straight up from the pool.'

'There's an abrasion on the front of the right thigh, where he was wedged,' supplemented the doctor.

'Yes, but that's natural. Those scratches aren't.'

'And there's another thing, though I didn't put this in my report because I'm not certain. I've an idea those lacerations were made during life. There were signs of free bleeding – freer than I should have expected after death.'

'That clinches it,' said Roger.

'Clinches what, sir?' asked the inspector.

The return of the chief constable prevented Roger from answering. Major Drake wore an air of triumph.

'Well, it seems we've caught a Tartar,' he announced. 'This fellow was wanted by the Yard for share-pushing. They've arrested his partner, but didn't know Hutton was here. They saw the report of the accident in this morning's papers.'

'Well, fancy that,' observed the inspector.

Roger stared down at the dead man. 'You never know, do you? He doesn't look like my idea of a share-pusher. Those long hands. Weak chin, too.'

'Yes, yes: criminal type, obviously,' pronounced the major. 'Well, doctor, this is bound to raise the question of suicide. Fellow wanted by the police and all that. Any chance, do you think?'

'I shouldn't have said so. But of course he may have swum deliberately too far out and drowned himself.'

'And Barton got drowned trying to save him,' suggested the superintendent. 'The papers might fake up something like that.'

Roger broke into the discussion.

'Look here, I'd better tell you. This man Hutton didn't commit suicide, or get drowned by accident. He was murdered.'

There was a pause.

'Really, Sheringham,' observed the chief constable with

ANTHONY BERKELEY

disgust. 'Didn't I warn you, Superintendent? Sheringham, this is no time for joking. We're due on the golf course in ten minutes.'

'What makes you think he was murdered, Mr Sheringham?' asked the superintendent, more temperately.

Roger explained, calling on the doctor for support. The chief constable was not convinced.

'Scratches! Nonsense! Bathing dress, that's all.'

'Do you mean, he wore a backless swimsuit, as I believe the loathsome term is?'

'He was wearing a pair of slips,' said the superintendent. 'They were a goodish bit torn at the back, but not in front.'

'It's murder,' said Roger with finality. 'And I think I know how it was done. I want Inspector Clarke to take me to where the body was found, and help me look round.'

'Inspector Clarke has his work to do,' barked the major.

'This is his work. And I warn you, if you don't take up an investigation of this case, I'll write an article for *The Daily Courier* showing how the murder was done, and blame the Penhampton police for obstruction.'

'I believe you would, too,' admitted the baffled chief constable. 'Very well. You can have Clarke for an hour or two this afternoon to help investigate your mare's nest. In the meantime—'

'Oh, I'm not playing golf,' Roger retorted. 'Come on, Inspector. If we hurry we can reach the major's car before he does.'

It was only a few minutes' run in the car from Penhampton to the place where the body had been found, about a mile and a half from Penmouth on the Penhampton side. The inspector took Roger down by a cliff path, and showed him the place on the rocky shore.

'Very convenient,' Roger commented. 'Would you say that a body washing about on the incoming tide could possibly wedge itself there?'

The inspector considered. 'Well, now that you mention it, sir—'

'Exactly. It was put there. Probably in the hope that it wouldn't be found for days. Now let me see, was the murder committed here, or not? Probably not, but certainly within a short distance. He wouldn't want to carry the body far.'

Roger looked around. The coast at this point consisted entirely of rock, with a short fringe of shingle round the cove; of the sand implied in its name there was none. The rock was tolerably flat, but sprinkled lavishly with heavy boulders and broken up by innumerable pools, big and small. Floor-rock and boulders were alike plastered with barnacles and seaweed.

'What exactly are you looking for, sir?' the inspector asked.

'A pool. Not as big as this one, but not too small. A pool that may not show any traces at all, for two tides have been over it already; but this time yesterday the pool I want was pink.'

'You think that he was murdered in a pool then, sir?' said the inspector curiously. 'Well, I don't see why, but there's one just over there.'

'Too big.'

'There's a smaller one just beyond it.'

'Too small.' Roger looked round carefully. On the seaward

side of a particularly large rock was a medium-sized, oblong-shaped pool. 'That's more like it. And hidden from the shore, you see. Let's have a look at that one.'

They slithered over the seaweed and rock and looked down into the serene water. There was nothing to be seen but the floating seaweed and the barnacles over the flattish bottom.

'Well, there's nothing else for it,' Roger sighed. 'I must get in. Any regulations here against bathing in the nude?'

'If there are, sir, I've forgotten them,' promised the inspector.

Roger undressed, balancing with difficulty on the seaweed, and stepped into the pool. The water came just to his knees.

'What do you expect to find, sir?'

'Probably nothing. I hoped there might be some signs of a struggle – seaweed torn off or something. As it is—' He began to grope carefully among the thick bunches of seaweed that lined the sides.

The inspector watched for a few minutes then let his eyes wander towards the shore. He could take advantage of the visit at any rate to obtain Barton's description from Mr Turner, the farmer. As to the murder, what on earth would a man like Barton want to murder Hutton for? Why, according to the information he had collected, they had only known each other a couple of days, after a chance encounter in the cove here. Then an idea came to him.

'You mean, Barton might have been one of Hutton's share-pushing victims, Mr Sheringham? Perhaps he followed him down here, to do him in.'

'There are all sorts of possibilities,' Roger said abstract-edly, from the depths of the pool. 'But I think – hullo! What's this?'

He groped for a minute, and then drew out a shining object through which a strand of seaweed still ran.

'A ring. A man's wedding ring.' He peered inside. '"E. H. – B. G. 18 November 1933". E. H. What was Hutton's Christian name, Inspector?'

'Edward, sir. Well, that proves it right enough.' The inspector did not withhold his admiration. 'A smart bit of work, sir, and that's a fact.'

'I thought I was on the right tack,' Roger said modestly and scrambled out of the pool.

While he dressed they discussed the next move. A visit to the farm was indicated, and another to the Hutton's lodg-ings. In the end it was decided that the inspector should go up to the farm and get Barton's description and any other particulars, while Roger had a look through the man's tent.

'And find out what clothes he usually wore,' he instructed the inspector.

'Yes, sir. Well, if you're ready – why, bless my soul, you've never told me how the murder was done.'

'As I suspected from the beginning. And,' Roger grinned, 'if you'd care to step into the pool with me, Inspector, I'd guarantee to murder you too, in less than two minutes, though you're a bigger man than me. No? Well, have you ever heard of the Brides in the Bath case?'

A light broke over the inspector, and shone in his face.

'Exactly,' Roger nodded. 'He got the man into the pool somehow – perhaps called his attention to that bunch of red anemones – then grabbed his ankles, hoisted his legs in the air so that his head went under the water, and in two minutes or less the job was done.'

'And but for those barnacles, sir—'

'Exactly. He'd have got away with it.'

*

The inspector was longer at the farm than Roger, waiting in the car, had expected, but when he returned he was brimming with news.

'The woman's in it, sir.'

'Ah! You've discovered that?'

'Did you know, Mr Sheringham?'

'I had a strong suspicion. Well, what have you learned?'

'Why, sir,' explained the inspector, 'by a stroke of luck I found a man who was working in this field yesterday afternoon. He says he saw a woman on the beach about half-past three, and the clothes he describes her as wearing tally well enough with Mrs Hutton's when she got to the station.'

'Mrs Hutton didn't mention being on the beach in the afternoon?'

'No, sir: she did not. But that's not all. There was a man with her.'

'The deuce there was!'

'Yes, sir. By the looks of it, they came out of a little cave under the cliff here. (I must have a look there later.) Manders – that's the farmhand – thought they might be a larky couple, so he watched; but after talking a minute the man went back into the cave, and the woman went off along the beach. Manders didn't see either of them again.'

'I see. And Barton's description?'

'Well, Mrs Turner couldn't tell me much. Average sort of height, she thought; not a big man. When she saw him on the day he arrived, the nineteenth, he had on a blue suit; afterwards he always wore a pullover and grey trousers.'

'A blue suit?' Roger repeated with interest. 'There's no blue suit in the tent now.'

'Ah!' said the inspector. 'And about Barton's moustache—'

'Barton has no moustache now,' Roger said impatiently.

'No, sir. Just what I was going to suggest. Because the chap Manders saw – he hadn't got a moustache either, but he was wearing a blue suit.'

Roger nodded, as if the news hardly surprised him.

'What do we do next, sir? This is your case.'

Roger thought.

'We go to the Hutton's lodging,' he said briskly.

'To interview Mrs Hutton?'

'No, no. Not yet. To look for a razor. You see, Barton's razor is here.'

The inspector looked puzzled. Then he beamed intelligently. 'I get you, sir. He ought to have taken it with him, but he couldn't risk coming back to the tent after he'd done the murder. He had his blue suit in the cave all ready, but he forgot his razor to shave off his moustache with. So Mrs Hutton—'

*

Mrs Wainwright, the stout, motherly lady who kept Ocean

View, was garrulous. She also wiped her eyes a great deal on her apron. Hutton had evidently been her star boarder. Roger listened with patience to her praise of him while the inspector was professionally busy upstairs.

'... a *real* gentleman, he was. So spick and span, and always ready with a joke. Oh, dear, it's sad to think he's gone. Not that he didn't like having things his own way: well, you can't blame a gentleman for that, can you? Not that she ever complained; not the complaining sort, Mrs Hutton isn't. And so well they got on. Never a cross word, that *I* heard. Of course he used to lay down the law a bit, but Mrs Hutton didn't mind that. One of the quiet ones, Mrs Hutton is. (But what she'll say if she comes now and finds the other police gentleman in her bedroom, I don't know. No lady would like that.)

'Upset, sir? Well, it's funny you should ask that, because to tell you the truth she does puzzle me a bit. In fact I'm blest if I've seen her cry yet. Well, it doesn't seem natural somehow, does it? Goes down to the beach with a book or some knitting, just like she used to. "You have a good cry," I tell her, "it'll do you good," but—

'Yes, she went back to the beach yesterday afternoon. Said she was just going to have another look round before she went to the police, poor soul. What's that, sir? No, no parcel. Just her beach bag, like she always carried; and—'

The arrival of the inspector cut short the flow.

In the car the two men exchanged results, and the inspector reported at once that no razor was to be found.

'That's what she went back to the beach for,' he said with satisfaction. 'To take him the razor. You see, Manders being

110

in the field above, Barton couldn't get back to his tent—
Sir!' exclaimed the inspector, aghast at his own perspicuity.
'Were they lovers, her and Barton? Is that why Barton killed
Hutton?' His face fell. 'Oh, but she said they'd only met
once.' He sighed, and then brightened up again. 'That's what
she *said*. But suppose they'd been lovers before? They both
come from London, you see. What do you think, sir?'

Roger smiled. 'What do I think? I think you had better
find out whether Hutton was insured. That's a more likely
line of enquiry.'

'Insured, eh?' The inspector whistled. 'You mean, Barton
was hard up, and she promised him a share of the insurance
money? Pretty quick work, with a comparative stranger.'

'Nevertheless,' Roger persisted, 'if Hutton hadn't been
insured, I'm pretty certain there'd have been no murder.'

*

At the police station the superintendent was still waiting for
them. On hearing their news he actually summoned the chief
constable from his sacred golf course.

With professional gallantry the latter first swallowed his
own words and then showed himself in such an amenable
state of mind that Roger was able without difficulty to obtain
permission on two points: that for the moment Mrs Hutton
would be kept in her state of happy ignorance, and that the
London police should be asked to bring down on Monday
morning Hutton's partner, now in custody, to answer a
few questions which Roger promised should be of the first
importance in solving the case.

'But what about Barton, sir?' the superintendent wanted to know. 'We must put out an enquiry for him.'

'Well, make it a confidential one, to the police only,' Roger conceded. 'The great thing is that Mrs Hutton must not be alarmed.'

For the rest of the weekend he refused to say a further word about the case, to the disappointment of his host.

The inquest had been fixed for Monday morning, but in view of the new developments only formal evidence of identification was taken and Mrs Hutton was the sole witness called, the coroner then adjourning the enquiry for three weeks. After the proceedings Mrs Hutton was invited to the police station to answer a few questions.

'What are you going to ask her?' Roger enquired of the superintendent, as they walked together from the schoolroom which had formed the Coroner's Court. The chief constable had not attended the inquest.

'Oh, just a few questions which she may find some difficulty in answering, Mr Sheringham.'

'Are you going to tell her that you know it's murder?'

'No, no. Not yet, sir. That would never do. We don't want to put the two of them on their guard.'

Mrs Hutton seemed nervous. She denied that she knew anything about the warrant issued for her husband's arrest, about his share-pushing activities, or about his insurance arrangements; she admitted having visited the beach in the afternoon of Friday, but strongly denied she had met any man there, or even seen one; she denied with equal vehemence that she had known Barton in London, or had ever had any conversation with him alone; she knew nothing about any missing razor of her husband's. But much of her denying lacked conviction, and her hesitations and evasions were obvious. Then she suddenly went hysterical, demanded to know why all these questions were being asked of her, and announced that she would answer no more. The chief constable sent her under the care of a sergeant into another room to recover.

'Pity, sir,' remarked the superintendent drily. 'She'd have spilled the beans in another minute.'

'Must play a game by its rules,' pointed out the chief constable. 'Well, Sheringham, what about her? She's in it, eh?'

'Oh, she's in it all right,' Roger agreed. 'Has that partner of Hutton's arrived, by the way?'

'Field? Yes. They've put him in one of the cells.'

Roger thought for a minute. 'Can we have Mrs Hutton back in about ten minutes? I should like to ask her just one question myself. In the meantime—' He scribbled something on a piece of paper which he gave to the superintendent.

The latter read it, raised his eyebrows, scratched his head, shrugged his shoulders, and then nodded; after which he rose and went out of the room. The chief constable, in confabulation with Inspector Clarke on the other side of the room, had noticed nothing. A minute later the superintendent slipped into his chair again.

The ten minutes passed slowly. At the end of them Mrs Hutton was brought back. She looked pale, but more composed and even defiant.

Roger leaned towards her.

'Mrs Hutton, you have identified the body you saw in the mortuary as that of your husband. Did you know that he had been brutally *murdered*?'

There was a moment's pandemonium. Mrs Hutton shrieked, the police officials gave utterance to indignant protests.

Roger waved the latter aside. 'It's part of my case,' he explained, 'that Mrs Hutton knows nothing of the murder.'

'I don't, I don't,' screamed the obviously distraught woman. 'It's not true.'

'It is true.' Roger went to the door and beckoned. A constable brought in a small man with a sharp, rat-like face.

Roger looked at him. 'You're Field? Well?'

'That's not Eddie Hutton, that stiff,' affirmed the rat-like stranger. 'Never seen him before in my puff.'

Roger signed to the constable to take him away.

'Well, Mrs Hutton?' he said.

This time the beans were well and truly spilled.

*

'I don't believe Hutton came down here intending murder,' Roger said, when the sobbing woman had been removed again.

'But the chance meeting with Barton was too much for him. He certainly had murder in his mind when he left his lodgings on Friday morning, with the razor to cut off Barton's moustache all ready in his pocket. (He ought to have shaved the chin too, by the way; that was what first made me smell a rat.) It was easy to deceive his wife into believing that both of them had got into difficulties in the water, and Barton had been accidentally drowned. Then he sprang the news of Field's arrest on her and the warrant for his own, and pointed out that this was his one chance if she would identify the body as his. He taught her the description of Barton, and she learned it by heart. There wasn't much risk, you see, in a place where he was a complete stranger; and as you know, it very nearly came off. Really, almost the only risk Hutton ran was in going up to Barton's tent to get that blue suit. It was clever, and so simple. The life insurance Mrs Hutton was to claim may not be huge, but it would be a nice sum to begin—'

The telephone-bell cut him short.

The superintendent listened, expressed his satisfaction, and hung up. 'They've got Hutton,' he announced. 'Just where she said he'd be. She gave him away properly, I'll say.'

'We caught her at the right moment,' Roger commented. 'Half an hour later, when the reaction set in, she might not have been so ready to give him away. By the way, what are you going to do with her?'

'Do with her? Why, we shall—'

'Exactly. What can you do? You can have her up for perjury, or conspiracy, or obstructing the police, but if she pleads coercion she'll certainly get off. Why not let her go?'

The chief constable snorted indignantly. The woman had led them all down the garden path, and it had taken a confounded amateur to—

'Let her go,' repeated Roger.

They let her go.

The Furies

Michael Innes

'The death of Miss Pinhorn,' said Appleby, 'was decidedly bizarre. But it was some time before we realised that it was sinister, too. Indeed, if it hadn't been for my aunt we might never have thought of it. She takes a great interest, you know, in criminal investigation.'

'I remember Miss Pinhorn slightly.' The vicar set down his tankard. 'My daughter called on her once when collecting for European relief. She owned a cottage here, I think, and so it appeared reasonable to treat her as a resident. But she opened her purse – in the actual rather than the metaphorical sense – and gave the poor girl sixpence.'

The doctor chuckled. 'Then you may take it she was stretching a point, and that your daughter's eloquence had moved her in uncommon degree. She was quite astonishingly mean. I was abroad when she died, and I don't know anything about her end. But I should guess that the chronic malnutrition of the pathological miser had a hand in it. Is that right?'

Appleby shook his head. 'Certainly she was terribly mean—and about her food among other things. She would have lived, if she could, on free samples of breakfast cereals. But she died, nevertheless, of something odder than starvation. In a sense she died of drink.'

'Dear, dear!' The vicar's features composed themselves momentarily upon strictly professional lines. 'It is a deplorable fact that elderly unmarried women—'

'And it was the drink that worried my aunt. She simply would not believe Miss Pinhorn capable of paying out good money for the pleasure of drinking two pints of beer as it is today. It worried me, too. There did seem to be something rather incredible about that beer. But I see I must tell the story.'

'Capital,' said the doctor. 'And we'll try a second pint ourselves.'

'Amelia Pinhorn was a woman of considerable fortune and marked eccentricity. But while she enjoyed the benefits of her fortune all the time, her eccentricity was intermittent. For most of the year she lived in London the normal life of a leisured person of her sort: two servants, a fixed circle of acquaintances, concert-going, church-going – that sort of thing. Then for a couple of months each summer she came down here – her parents had been Sheercliffe folk – and led a solitary and miserly existence in a small cottage not half a mile from where we are sitting now. She had no contacts with anybody – not even the milkman. I don't exaggerate. Everything was sent down from town before she arrived.

She lived on tins. It was said that she believed the Sheercliffe shopkeepers to be peculiarly malignant, and eager to poison her. In all this there is, perhaps, nothing very out of the way. Here was an old woman who had formed the habit of concentrating a tendency towards mild insanity within a two months' spell at the sea, when she lived alone and was a nuisance to nobody. It was a public-spirited and rather heroic disposition of things. I used to see her taking her daily walk along the cliff – a handsome grey-haired woman, not carelessly or strangely dressed, but talking to herself in some withdrawn state that was decidedly alarming. And then one day she was drowned.'

'Drowned?' The doctor looked surprised. 'It sounds a bit of an anti-climax. Unless you mean that somebody drowned her in those two pints of beer?'

Appleby shook his head. 'The beer was an agent, not a medium. Miss Pinhorn simply tumbled into the sea and was drowned. Or at least it is supposed that she was drowned. For we never, you see, recovered the body. The poor lady went over the cliff just short of the lighthouse. You must know about the current that sweeps in there and then goes out to sea again past the Furies. Two or three times in a century the thing happens. If a body goes through there at a certain depth it gets sucked right down and trapped in nobody knows what monstrous system of submarine caverns lying beneath those three placid-looking pinnacles. And poor Miss Pinhorn passed that way. Which meant that all the king's dolphins and all the king's divers couldn't between them have dredged her up for a coroner's jury to sit upon. And this was awkward when the rumours began to go round. It might have been particularly awkward for Jane Pinhorn. Old women over their teacups would have credited the poor girl with the most masterly crime of the age.'

The vicar looked disturbed. 'This is not *really* a crime story, I hope?'

'It certainly is – but whether masterly or not, you must judge. The initial facts were perfectly simple, and fell within the observation of a number of people who were about here at the time. Miss Pinhorn emerged from her cottage, locked the door behind her, and set out on what appeared to be one of her normal solitary rambles. She came in the direction of this pub, and as she neared it she was seen to be hurrying – like a seasoned toper, somebody said, who is afraid of being beaten to it by closing time. But she wasn't known to drink, and she had certainly never been in this very comfortable private bar before. Well, in she came, talking to herself as usual and looking quite alarmingly wild. She called for two pints of beer in quick succession, floored them, planked down half a crown, and bolted out again. By this time she was singing and throwing her arms about.

'If the few people here had possessed any gumption they'd have followed the old girl and seen that she did herself no mischief. But she was known to be a bit dotty, and they hung back. Besides, she appeared to be making for home again. It was only when she had gone some way that she appeared to lose direction and wheel round towards the brow of the cliff. By that time she was in a thoroughgoing state of mania, and she went straight to her death. Perhaps, you may say, she had a repressed tendency to suicide – we found out afterwards that her father had made away with himself – and the need for that took charge when her inhibitions were destroyed by the poison. For this is a story of poisoning – as you, doctor, have no doubt realised.

'I've said that my aunt was the first person to suspect foul play. That needs qualifying, maybe. For the notion of poisoning seems to have arisen almost at once at what you might call a folk level. Everybody was whispering it, and on no very ponderable evidence. You may remember how it was believed that poor Miss Pinhorn was *afraid* of being poisoned. That may or may not have been true. I should be inclined to call it an aetiological myth – one invented for the purpose of accounting for an observed fact: namely, that Miss Pinhorn would buy neither food nor drink locally. What my aunt certainly spotted was the significance of the beer. It indicated, she said, a sudden pathological thirst. Together with the very rapid onset of a violent mania or delirium, it should give us a very good guide to the sort of poison at work.

'When I say "us" I mean, of course, the local police and myself. It's a queer thing that I seldom quit Scotland Yard to spend a week in Sheercliffe with my eminently respectable kinswoman without her involving me in something of a busman's holiday. But I felt bound to peer about. For a very little thought suggested to me that my aunt – in this instance at least – was talking sense. Had the body been recoverable I'd never have bothered my head. It was the fact that we had in that quarter an absolutely unknown x, so to speak, that got me really interested.

'Well, the first question clearly concerned the possibility of Miss Pinhorn's having poisoned herself, whether inadvertently or of set purpose. Her cottage was not a difficult place to search thoroughly – I shall come to that in a moment – and the hunt yielded what seemed at first a significant result. There was a tremendous store of patent medicines – something quite out of the way even with a maiden lady – all put up in very small packs. But each was more utterly harmless than the last. They were, in fact, almost without exception, free samples which had been stored away for a long time. I doubt if one can get very much in that way nowadays.

'A related enquiry to this was that into the dead woman's recent medical history. There was something of a hold-up over this, because in such matters she had been of a decidedly secretive habit. We did learn from her maids in town, however, that a few months previously she had been having trouble with her eyes, and that for some unknown reason she had to be hurried off to a nursing home. I ought to have seen a bit of light when I heard that.' Appleby paused. 'I can see, Doctor, that it at once conveys something to you.'

The doctor shook his head. 'Perhaps so. But I can't say that I see much sense—'

'Exactly.' Appleby applied himself briefly to the pewter mug before him. 'And what you might call the irony of this queer yarn lies just there. But now I must tell you about the chocolates.

'You see, it really comes down to a sort of sealed-room mystery. Miss Pinhorn is poisoned – and yet *nothing* has gone into her cottage for days. Or so we thought until I happened, during the search, to take a second look at this half-pound box of chocolates. It was lying in the sitting room, with the

top layer gone. It wasn't anything about the chocolates themselves that struck me. It was the lid. You know that slightly
padded sort of lid that confectioners go in for? It was of that
kind. And just visible on it was the impress of three or four
parallel wavy lines. That box had been through the post,
lightly wrapped, and here was a faint trace of the postmark.'

'Most astonishing!' The vicar was enthusiastic. 'My dear
Appleby, a fine feat of detection, indeed.'

'I don't know that I'd call it that. But at least it sent me
to the wastepaper basket. And there, sure enough, with a
London postmark and Miss Pinhorn's address, was the scrap
of wrapping I expected. And there was something more – a
slip of notepaper with the words: "To Aunt Amelia on her
birthday, with love from Jane."

'So I hunted out the postman. Apart from a few letters, he
had delivered nothing at Miss Pinhorn's for weeks – until the
very morning of the day on which she died. On that day he
had delivered a small oblong parcel.

'I looked like being hot on a trail. That evening, while
the remaining chocolates were being analysed with what was
to prove an entirely negative result, I went up to town and
sought out Jane Pinhorn. And I didn't care for what I found.
Jane was as nice a girl as you could wish to meet, and she had
liked her eccentric aunt. This birthday box of chocolates had
been an annual occasion with her. She was a highly intelligent girl, too.

'Miss Pinhorn's symptoms, so far as we knew about them,
were consistent with the ingestion of some poison of the
atropine group. The sudden thirst, and the delirium result-
ing from incoordinate stimulation of the higher centres of

the cerebrum, were consistent with this. Deadly nightshade, as you may know, is not in fact all that deadly. But one could no doubt cram a chocolate with quite enough to cause a great deal of mischief, and Jane Pinhorn had possessed the opportunity to do this. Moreover she had a motive. Along with a male cousin – a ne'er-do-well in Canada – she was the dead woman's only relative and co-heir. I saw suspicion inevitably attaching itself to this girl. It was overwhelmingly unlikely, indeed, that any case against her could be proved. But that was a matter of the sheerest chance. Miss Pinhorn's body had gone forever – a thing the girl could not possibly have reckoned on. As a crime of intelligence and calculation the thing would not do. The sealed-room aspect of Miss Pinhorn's way of living while at Sheercliffe, and the penetrating of the defences thus created by this single gift which was so easily traceable to the sender: it just didn't make sense – unless indeed Jane Pinhorn had a repressed suicidal strain herself.

'I came back to Sheercliffe that night seriously troubled, and as soon as I arrived I went straight out to the dead woman's cottage. It was locked and sealed, but I had been given a key. The rest of that night – and I remember it as very long – I spent prowling from one room to another hunting for I didn't know what. Essentially I was casting about inside my own head for some logic in the thing that had escaped me. I don't think I had any notion of hitting upon a further material clue. And then, quite suddenly, I found that I had come to a halt in the little hall and was staring at an envelope lying beside the telephone directory on a small table. It was a plain manilla envelope, stamped ready for post, and creased down the middle. For a second I didn't see the significance of that crease. What had touched off some spring in my mind was the address – a single-spaced typescript affair of the most commonplace sort. *International Vitamin Warehouses Limited*, if mildly absurd, was nothing out of the way and wouldn't have troubled me. The snag lay in what followed. I know my East London fairly well. And the street in which this pretentious organisation claimed an abode contains nothing but mean private houses and a few shabby little shops. And so the truth came to me … The truth, to begin with, about that crease. This envelope had come to Miss Pinhorn folded inside another one.

'I slit the thing open there and then. *"Send no money. Simply fill up the back of this form …"* It had been a diabolically clever scheme. And it had, of course, been a completely fatuous one as well.'

Appleby paused. The vicar was looking largely puzzled. But the doctor drew a long breath. 'The nephew in Canada!'

'Precisely. He knew about the sealed-room effect. He knew about Jane's annual birthday gift. And he knew about his aunt's idiosyncrasy to belladonna. Some months before, its use by her oculist in a normal clinical dose had made her so seriously unwell as to take her into a nursing home. He believed that he could get on the gum of a reply-paid envelope a quantity which in her special case would be fatal. Miss Pinhorn, you remember, could never resist a free sample of anything. So she would fill in the form, lick the envelope – and perish! There are Elizabethan plays, you know, rather like that; people die in them quite horribly after kissing a poisoned portrait. The envelope, if posted, would go to what was in fact a shady accommodation address in London, and our precious nephew would pick it up when he came over to England. He would also pick up the half of his aunt's fortune – or the whole of it if the unfortunate Jane was hanged on the strength of her chocolates.

'In point of fact, however many wicked nephews you may have in Canada, you need never have any qualms about licking an envelope doped with belladonna. Or rather, qualms are all that you *will* have. This amateur in poison had sadly confused a lethal with a toxic dose. With this particular drug, as it happens, the margin between the two is unusually wide. Having her special susceptibility to it, poor old Miss Pinhorn did go horribly delirious, just as she had on a previous occasion. But that she chose to hurry on to this pub near the cliff, and thus put herself in the way of tumbling into the sea when the attack was at its worst, was pure chance.'

Appleby paused and stood up. 'It wasn't, as it happened, the last stroke of chance in the Pinhorn case. You may wonder what happened to the nephew.'

The vicar nodded vigorously. 'Yes, indeed. He was certainly a murderer.'

'He had aimed at being that, and he showed a certain efficiency. From a small town in Canada he had timed his stroke so nicely that the bogus circular reached his aunt just when he intended: on her birthday, and when Jane Pinhorn's customary chocolates would be arriving too.

'But he hadn't the stuff that an effective killer is made of. No sooner had he set his plot in motion, it seems, than he cracked up badly and went on a drinking bout. Staggering home one morning in the small hours, and making his way through some public park, he fell into a very small pond and was drowned in six inches of water. At just about the same hour, that tremendous current must have been drawing Amelia Pinhorn's body to unknown depths beneath the Furies.'

Daisy Bell

Gladys Mitchell

Daisy, Daisy, give me your answer, do!
I've gone crazy, all for the love of you!
It won't be a stylish marriage,
We can't afford a carriage,
But you'll look neat upon the seat
Of a bicycle made for two.

In the curved arm of the bay the sea lay perfectly still. Towards the horizon was reflected back the flashing light of the sun, but under the shadow of huge cliffs the dark-green water was as quiet as a lake at evening.

Above, riding over a ridge between two small villages, went the road, a dusty highway once, a turnpike on which the coach had changed horses three times in twenty miles. That dusty road was within the memory of the villagers; in the post office there were picture postcards, not of the coaches, certainly, but of the horse-drawn station bus on the shocking gradients and hairpin bends of the highway.

The road was now slightly wider – not much, because every extra foot had to be hacked from the rocky hillside, for on one side the road fell almost sheer to the sea. A humped turf edge kept this seaward boundary (insufficiently, some said, for there had been motoring accidents, especially in the dark), and beyond the humped edge, and, treacherously, just out of sight of motorists who could see the rolling turf but not the danger, there fell away a Gadarene descent of thirteen hundred feet.

George took the road respectfully, with an eye for hairpin bends and (although he found this irksome) an occasional toot on the horn. His employer, small, spare and upright, sat beside him, the better to admire the rolling view. Equally with the moorland scenery she admired her chauffeur's driving. She was accustomed to both phenomena, but neither palled on her. In sixteen crawling miles she had not had a word to say.

At the County Boundary, however, she turned her head slightly to the right.

'The next turning, George. It's narrow.'

His eyes on the road ahead, the chauffeur nodded, and the car turned off to the left down a sandy lane, at the bottleneck of which it drew up courteously in face of a flock of lively, athletic, headstrong moorland sheep. The shepherd saluted Mrs Bradley, passed the time of day with the chauffeur, said it was a pity all they motors shouldn't have the same danged sense, and urged his charges past the car, and kept them within some sort of bounds with the help of a shaggy dog.

At the bottom of the slope, and wedged it seemed in the

hollow, was a village with a very small church. Mrs Bradley went into the churchyard to inspect the grave of an ancestress (she believed) of her own who had died in the odour of sanctity, but, if rumour did not lie, only barely so, for she had enjoyed a reputation as a witch.

Mrs Bradley, looking (with her black hair, sharp black eyes, thin hands, and beaky little mouth) herself not at all unlike a witch, spent an interesting twenty minutes or so in the churchyard, and then went into the church.

Its architectural features were almost negligible. A fourteenth-century chancel (probably built on the site of the earliest church), a badly restored nave, a good rood screen, and the only remaining bit of Early English work mutilated to allow for an organ loft, were all obvious. There seemed, in fact, very little, on a preliminary investigation, to interest even the most persistent or erudite visitor.

In the dark south wall, however, of what had been the Lady Chapel, Mrs Bradley came upon a fourteenth-century piscina whose bowl had been carved in the likeness of a hideous human head. She took out a magnifying glass and examined the carving closely. Montague Rhodes James, with his genius for evoking unquiet imaginings and terrifying, atavistic fears, might have described the expression upon its horrid countenance. All that Mrs Bradley could accomplish was a heathenish muttering indicative of the fact that, in her view, the countenance betrayed indication of at least two major Freudian complexes and a Havelock Ellis regression into infantile criminology.

'A murderer's face, ma'am,' said a voice behind her. 'Ay, as I stand, that be a murderer's face.'

She turned and saw the verger with his keys. 'Ay, they do tell, and vicar he do believe it, as carver was vouchsafed a true, just vision of Judas Iscariot the traitor, and carved he out for all to look upon.'

He smiled at her – almost with the sinister leer of the carving itself, thought Mrs Bradley, startled by the change in his mild and previously friendly expression. He passed on into the vestry, dangling his keys.

Shaking her head, Mrs Bradley dropped some money into the offertory box on the pillar nearest the porch, and took the long sloping path between the headstones of the graves to the lych-gate. Here she found George in conversation with a black-haired woman. George had always given himself (with how much truth his employer had never troubled herself to find out) the reputation of being a misogynist, and on this occasion, seated on the step of the car, he was, in his own phrase, 'laying down the law' with scornful masculine firmness. The girl had her back to the lych-gate. She was plump and bareheaded, and was wearing brown corduroy shorts, a slightly rucked-up blouse on elastic at the waist, and – visible from the back view which Mrs Bradley had of her – a very bright pink vest which showed between the rucked-up blouse and the shorts. For the rest she was brown-skinned and, seen face to face, rather pretty.

A tandem bicycle, built to accommodate two men, was resting against the high, steep, ivy-grown bank of the lane. The young woman, seeing Mrs Bradley, who had in fact strolled round to get a view of her, cut short George's jeremiads by thanking him. Then she walked across the road, set the tandem upright, pushed it sharply forward, and, in spite of the fact that the slope of the road was against her, mounted with agility and ease on to the front saddle. Then she tacked doggedly up the hill, the tandem, lacking any weight on the back seat, wagging its tail in what looked to Mrs Bradley a highly dangerous manner as it zigzagged up to the bend in the lane and wobbled unwillingly round it.

George had risen to his feet upon the approach of his employer, and now stood holding the door open.

'A courageous young woman, George?' suggested Mrs Bradley, getting into the car.

'A foolish one, madam, in my opinion,' George responded primly, 'and so I was saying to her when she was asking the way. Looking for trouble I call it to cycle one of them things down these roads. Look at the hill she's coming to, going to Lyndale this route. Meeting her husband, she says; only been married a month, and having their honeymoon now and using the tandem between them; him having to work thereabouts, and her cycling that contraption down from London, where she's living with her mother while he gets the home for her. Taken three days to do it in, and meeting him on top of Lyndale Hill this afternoon. More like a suicide pact, if you ask me what I think.'

'I not only ask you, George, but I am so much enthralled by what you think that I propose we take the same route and follow her.'

'We were due to do so in any case, madam, if I can find a place to turn the car in this lane.'

It took him six slow miles to find a suitable place. During the drive towards the sea, the big car brushing the summer hedgerows almost all the time, Mrs Bradley observed, 'I don't like to think of that young woman, George. I hope you advised her to wheel the bicycle on all dangerous parts of the road?'

'As well advise an errand boy to fit new brake-blocks, madam,' George austerely answered. 'I did advise her to that effect, but not to cut any ice. She fancies herself on that jigger. You can't advise women of that age.'

'Did you offer her any alternative route to Lyndale?'

'Yes, madam; not with success.'

At the top of the winding hill he turned to the left, and then, at the end of another five miles and a quarter of wind and the screaming seabirds, great stretches of moorland heather, bright green tracks of little peaty streams, and, south of the moor, the far-off ridges and tors, he engaged his lowest gear again and the car crept carefully down a long, steep, dangerous hill. There were warning notices on either side of the road, and the local authority, laying special emphasis on the subject of faulty brakes, had cut a parking space from the edge of the stubborn moor. The gradient of the steepest part of the hill was one in four. The car took the slant like a cat in sight of a bird.

'What do you think of our brakes, George?' Mrs Bradley enquired. George replied, in the reserved manner with which he received her more facetious questions, that the brakes were in order, or had been when the car was brought out of the garage.

'Well, then, pull up,' said his employer. 'Something has happened on the seaward side of the road. I think someone's gone over the edge.'

Her keen sight, and a certain sensitivity she had to visual

impressions, had not deceived her. She followed the track of a bicycle to the edge of the cliff, crouched, lay flat, and looked over.

Below her the seagulls screamed, and, farther down, the sea flung sullenly, despite the brilliant day, against the heavy rocks, or whirlpooled, snarling, about the black island prom-ontories, for the tide was on the turn and coming in fast. Sea-pinks, some of them brown and withered now, for their season was almost past, clung in the crevices or grew in the smallest hollows of the cliff-face. Near one root of them a paper bag had lodged. Had it been empty, the west wind, blowing freshly along the face of the cliff (which looked north to the Bristol Channel), must have removed it almost as soon as it alighted, but there it perched, not wedged, yet heavy enough to hold its place against the breeze. To the left of it, about four yards off, was a deep, dark stain, visible because it was on the only piece of white stone that could be seen.

'Odd,' said Mrs Bradley, and began to perform the feat which she would not have permitted to anyone under her control – that of climbing down to reach the dark-stained rock.

The stain was certainly blood, and was still slightly sticky to the touch. She looked farther down (having, fortunately, a mountaineer's head for heights) and thought that, some thirty feet below her, she could see a piece of cloth. It was caught on the only bush which seemed to have found root and sustenance upon the rocky cliff. It resembled, she thought, material of which a man's suit might be made.

She left it where it was and scrambled across to the bag.

'George,' she said, when she had regained the dark, overhanging lip of the rough turf edge of the cliff and had discovered her chauffeur at the top, 'I think I saw a public telephone marked on the map. Somebody ought to search the shore below these cliffs, I rather fancy.'

'It would need to be by boat, then, madam. The tide comes up to the foot,' replied the chauffeur. He began to walk back up the hill.

Mrs Bradley sat down at the roadside and waited for him to return. While she was waiting she untwisted the top of the screwed-up paper bag and examined the contents with interest.

She found a packet of safety-razor blades, a tube of tooth-paste half-full, a face flannel, a wrapped cake of soap of the dimensions known euphemistically in the advertisements as 'guest-size', a very badly worn toothbrush, a set of small buttons on a card, a pipe-cleaner, half a bicycle bell, two rubber patches for mending punctures and a piece of worm-like valve-rubber.

'Calculated to indicate that whoever left the bag there was a cyclist, George,' she observed, when her chauffeur came back from the telephone. 'Of course, nobody may have fallen over the cliff, but – what do you make of the marks?'

'Palmer tyres, gent's model – not enough clearance for a lady's – see where the pedal caught the edge of the turf?'

'Yes, George. Unfortunately one loses the track a yard from the side of the road. I should have supposed that the bicycle would have left a better account of itself if it had really been ridden over. Besides, what could have made anybody ride it over the edge? The road is wide enough, and there does not seem to be much traffic. I think perhaps I'll retrieve that piece of cloth before we go.'

'I most seriously hope you will not, madam, if you'll excuse me. I've no head for heights myself or I would get it. After all, we know just where it is. The police could get it later, with ropes and tackle for their men, if it *should* be required at an inquest.'

'Very true, George. Let us get on to the village to see whether a boat has put out. How much farther is it?'

'Another three miles and a half, madam. There's another hill after this – a smaller one.'

The car descended decorously. The hill dropped sheer and steep for about another half mile, and then it twisted suddenly away to the right, so that an inn which was on the left-hand side at the bend appeared, for an instant, to be standing in the middle of the road.

So far as the black-haired girl on the smashed and buckled tandem was concerned, that was where it might as well have stood, Mrs Bradley reflected. The tandem had been ridden straight into a brick wall – slap into it as though the rider had been blind or as though the machine she was riding had been completely out of her control. Whatever the cause of the accident, she had hurtled irrevocably to her death, or so Mrs Bradley thought when first she knelt beside her.

'Rat-trap pedals, of all things, madam,' said George. The plump large feet in the centre-seamed cycling shoes were still caught in the bent steel traps. George tested the brakes.

'The brakes don't act,' he said. 'Perhaps a result of the accident, madam, although I shouldn't think so.' He released the girl's feet and lifted the tandem away. Mrs Bradley, first delicately and then with slightly more firmness, sought for injuries.

'George,' she said, 'the case of instruments. And then go and get some cold water from somewhere or other.'

The girl had a fractured skull. Her left leg was slightly lacerated, but it was not bruised and the bone was not broken. Her face was unmarked, except by the dirt from the roadside. It was all a little out of the ordinary, Mrs Bradley thought, seizing the Thermos flask full of icy water which the resourceful George had brought from a moorland stream.

'She's alive, George, I think,' she said. 'But there have been some very odd goings-on. Are the tandem handlebars locked?'

'No, madam. They move freely.'

'Don't you think the front wheel should have been more seriously affected?'

'Why, yes, perhaps it should, madam. The young woman can't go much less than ten or eleven stone, and with the brakes out of order ...'

'And although her feet were caught in the rat-trap pedals, her face isn't even marked. It was only a little dirty before I washed it.'

'Sounds like funny business, madam, to me.'

'And to me, too. George. Is there a hospital near? We must have an ambulance if possible. I don't think the car will do. She ought to lie flat. That skull wants trepanning and at once. Mind how you go down the hill, though. I'll stay here with her. You might leave me a fairly heavy spanner.'

Left alone with the girl, Mrs Bradley fidgeted with her case of instruments, took out gouge forceps, sighed, shook her head, and put them back again. The wound on the top of the head was extremely puzzling. A fracture of the base of the skull would have been the most likely head injury, unless the girl had crashed head first into the wall, but, from the position in which the body had been lying, this seemed extremely unlikely. One other curious point Mrs Bradley noticed which changed her suppositions into certainty. The elastic-waisted white blouse and the shorts met neatly. It was impossible to believe that they could do so unless they had been pulled together after the girl had fallen from the saddle.

Mrs Bradley made a mental picture of the girl leaning forward over the low-slung sports-type handlebars of the machine. She must, in the feminine phrase, have 'come apart' at the back. That blouse could never have overlapped those shorts.

Interested and curious, Mrs Bradley turned up the edge of the soiled white blouse. There was nothing underneath it but the bare brown skin marked with two or three darker moles at the waist. Of the bright pink vest there was no sign; neither had the girl a knapsack or any kind of luggage into which she could have stuffed the vest supposing that she had taken it off for coolness.

'Odd,' said Mrs Bradley again, weighing the spanner thoughtfully in her hand. 'I wonder what's happened to the husband?'

At this moment there came round the bend an AA scout wheeling a bicycle. He saluted as he came nearer.

'Oh dear, madam! Nasty accident here! Poor young woman! Anything I can do?'

'Yes,' said Mrs Bradley very promptly. 'Get an ambulance.

I'm afraid she's dead, but there might be a chance if you're quick. No, don't touch her. I'm a doctor. I've done all that can be done here. Hurry, please. Every moment is important.'

'No ambulance in the village, madam. Couldn't expect it, could you? I might perhaps be able to get a car. How did you get here? Was you with her when she crashed?'

'Go and get a car. A police car, if you like. Dead or alive, she'll have to be moved as soon as possible.'

'Yes, she will, won't she?' said the man. He turned his bicycle, and, mounting it, shot away round the bend.

Mrs Bradley unfolded an Ordnance Survey map of the district and studied it closely. Then she took out a reading glass and studied it again. She put out a yellow claw and traced the line of the road she was on, and followed it into the village towards which first George and then the AA scout had gone.

The road ran on uncompromisingly over the thin red contour lines of the map, past nameless bays on one side and the shoulder of the moor on a rising hill on the other. Of deviations from it there were none; not so much as the dotted line of a moorland track, not even a stream, gave any indication that there might be other ways of reaching the village besides crossing the open moorland or keeping to the line of the road. There was nothing marked on the map but the cliffs and the shore on the one hand, the open hill country on the other.

She was still absorbed when George returned with the car.

'The village has no ambulance, madam, but the bus has decanted its passengers onto the bridge and is getting here as fast as it can. It was thought in the village, madam, that the body could be laid along one of the seats.'

'I hope and trust that "body" is but a relative term. The young woman will live, George, I fancy. Somebody has had his trouble for nothing.'

'I am glad to hear that, madam. The villagers seem well-disposed, and the bus is the best they can do.'

He spoke of the villagers as though they were the aboriginal inhabitants of some country which was still in the process of being explored. Mrs Bradley gave a harsh little snort of amusement and then observed, 'Did the AA scout stop and speak to you? Or did you ask him for information?'

'No, madam, neither at all. He was mending a puncture when I passed him.'

'Was that on your journey to the village or on the return here?'

'Just now, madam. I saw no one on my journey to the village.'

'Interesting,' said Mrs Bradley, thinking of her Ordnance map. 'Punctures are a nuisance, George, are they not? If you see him again you might ask him whether *Daisy Bell* met her husband on top of the hill.'

Just then the bus arrived. Off it jumped a police sergeant and a constable, who, under Mrs Bradley's direction, lifted the girl and placed her on one of the seats, of which the bus had two, running the whole of the inside length of the vehicle.

'You take the car to the hotel, George. I'll be there as soon as I can,' said his employer. 'Now, constable, we have to hold her as still as we can. Sergeant, kindly instruct the driver to avoid the bumps in the road, and then come in here and hold my coat to screen the light from her head. Is there a hospital in the village?'

'No, ma'am. There's a home for inebriates, though. That's the nearest thing. We're going to take her there, and Constable Fogg is fetching Doctor MacBain.'

'Splendid,' said Mrs Bradley, and devoted herself thenceforward entirely to her patient.

One morning some days later, when the mist had cleared from the moors and the sun was shining on every drop of moisture, she sent for the car, and thus addressed her chauffeur:

'Well, did you give the scout my message?'

'Yes, madam, but he did not comprehend it.'

'Indeed? And did you explain?'

'No, madam, not being instructed.'

'Excellent, child. We shall drive to the fatal spot, and there we shall see – what we shall see.'

George, looking haughty because he felt befogged, held open the door of the car, and Mrs Bradley put her foot on the step.

'I'll sit in front, George,' she said.

The car began to mount slowly to the bend where the accident had come to their notice. George was pulling up, but his employer invited him to go on.

'Our goal is the top of the hill, George. That is where they were to meet, you remember. That is the proper place from which to begin our enquiry. Is it not strange and interesting to consider all the motives for murder and attempted murder that come to men's minds? To women's minds, too, of course. The greater includes the less.'

She cackled harshly. George who (although he would have found it difficult to account for his opinion) had always conceived her to be an ardent feminist, looked at the road ahead, and did not relax his expression of dignified aloofness.

Prevented, by the fact that he was driving, from poking him in the ribs (her natural reaction to an attitude such as the one he was displaying), Mrs Bradley grinned tigerishly, and the car crawled on up the worst and steepest part of the gradient.

George then broke his silence.

'In my opinion, madam, no young woman losing her brakes on such a hill could have got off so light as *she* did, nor that tandem either.'

'True, George.'

'If you will excuse the question, madam, what put the idea of an attempt on her into your mind?'

'I suppose the piscina, George.'

George concluded that she was amusing herself at his expense and accepted the reply for what it was worth, which to him was nothing, since he did not know what a piscina was (and was habitually averse to seeking such information). He drove on a little faster as the gradient eased to one in seven and then to one in ten.

'Just here, George,' said his employer. 'Run off on to the turf on the right-hand side.'

George pulled up very close to the A A telephone which he had used before. Here the main road cut away from the route they had traversed and an A A scout was on duty at the junction.

'"*Behind the barn, down on my knees*,"' observed Mrs Bradley, chanting the words in what she fondly believed to be accents of their origin, "*I thought I heard a chicken sneeze*" – and I did, too. Come and look at this, George.'

It was the bright pink vest. There was no mistaking it, although it was stained now, messily and rustily, with blood.

'Not *her* blood, George; *his*,' remarked Mrs Bradley. 'I wonder he dared bring it back here, all the same. And I wonder where the young woman the first time fell off the tandem?' She looked again at the bloodstained vest. 'He must have cut himself badly, but, of course, he had to get enough blood to make the white stone look impressive, and he wanted the vest to smear it on with so that he need use nothing of his own. Confused thinking, George, on the whole, but murderers do think confusedly, and one can feel for them, of course.'

She sent George to fetch the AA scout, who observed, 'Was it the young woman as fell off bottom of Countsferry? Must have had a worse tumble just here by the box than Stanley seemed to think. He booked the tumble in his private log. Would you be the young woman's relatives, ma'am?'

'We represent her interests,' said Mrs Bradley, remarking afterwards to George that she thought they might consider themselves as doing so since they had saved her life.

'Well, he's left the log with me, and it do seem to show the cause of her shaking up. Must have been dazed like, and not seen the bend as it was coming, and run herself into the wall. And Stanley, they do say, must have gone over the cliff in trying to save her, for he ain't been back on duty any more. Cruel, these parts, they be.'

'Did her fall upset both her brakes, then?' Mrs Bradley enquired. She read the laconic entry in the exercise book presented for her inspection and, having earned the scout's gratitude in the customary simple manner, she returned to the car with the vest (which the scout had not seen) pushed into the large pocket of her skirt.

'Stop at the scene of the accident, George,' she said. 'She seemed,' said George admiringly later on to those who were standing him a pint in exchange for the story, 'like a blood-hound on the murderer's trail.'

'For a murderer he was, in intention, if not in fact,' continued George, taking, without his own knowledge, a recognised though debatable ecclesiastical view. 'She climbed up the bank and onto the moor as if she knew just what to look for, madam did. She showed me the very stone she reckoned he hit the young woman over the head with, and then where he sunk in the soft earth deeper than his first treads, because he was carrying the body back to the tandem to make out she crashed and fell off.'

'And didn't she crash?' his hearers wanted to know.

'Crash? What, her? A young woman who, to give her her due (although I don't hold with such things), had cycled that tandem – sports model and meant for two men – all the way down there from London? No. He crashed the tandem himself after he'd done her in. That was to deceive the police or anybody else that found her. He followed her on his bike down the hill with the deed in his heart. You see, he was her husband.

'But he didn't deceive me and madam, not by a long chalk he didn't! Why, first thing I said to her, I said, "Didn't it ought to be buckled up more than that if she came down that hill without brakes?" Course, that was his little mistake. That, and using her vest. I hope they give him ten years!

'Well, back we went up the hill to where madam found the

paper bag and its etceteras. The only blood we could see was on the only white stone.'

The barmaid at this point begged him to stop. He gave her the horrors, she said.

'So what?' one listener enquired.

'Well, the whole bag of tricks was to show that *someone*, and that someone a man and a cyclist, had gone over the cliff and was killed, like the other scout said. That was going to be our scout's alibi if the police ever got on his track, so madam thinks, but he hoped he wouldn't need to use that; it was just his standby, like. The other AA man had seen him go off duty. That was his danger, or so he thought, not reckoning on madam and me. He'd fixed the head of the young woman's machine while she stood talking to him at the AA telephone, so that when she mounted it threw her. That was to show (that's why he logged it, see?) as she mightn't have been herself when she took the bend. Pretty little idea.'

Three days later Mrs Bradley said to him, 'They will be able to establish motive at the trial, George. Bell – I call him that – was arrested yesterday evening. He had insured his wife, it appears, as soon as they were married, and wished to obtain possession of the money.'

'But what I would still like to know, madam,' George observed, 'is what put the thought of murder into your mind before ever we saw the accident or even the bag and the blood.'

'The bag and the blood, for some reason, sounds perfectly horrible, George.'

'But, madam, you spotted the marks he'd made on that edge with his push-bike as though you'd been *waiting* to spot them. And you fixed on him as the murderer, too, straight away.'

'Ah, that was easy, George. You see, he never mentioned that he'd seen you go by in the car, and you told me that on your journey to the village to find assistance you had not seen him either. Therefore, since he must have been somewhere along that road, I asked myself why, even if he should have left the roadside himself, his bicycle should not have been visible. Besides, he was the perfect answer to several questions which, up to that time, I had had to ask myself. One was: why did they choose to meet at the top of that hill? Another was: why did he risk bending over the injured girl to fix her feet back in those rat-trap pedals we saw and out of which, I should imagine, her feet would most certainly have been pulled if she'd had such a very bad crash?'

'Ah, yes, the AA box and the AA uniform, madam. In other words, Mr G. K. Chesterton's postman all over again.'

'Precisely, George. The obvious meeting place, in the circumstances, and the conspicuous yet easily forgotten uniform.'

'But, madam, if I may revert, what *did* turn your mind to murder?'

'The piscina, George,' Mrs Bradley solemnly reminded him.

George looked at her, hesitated, then overrode the habit of years and enquired, 'What is a piscina, madam?'

'A drain, George. Merely a drain.

'"Now, body, turn to air,

Or Lucifer will bear thee quick to hell!

O soul, be chang'd into little water drops,

And fall into the ocean, ne'er be found!"'

147

A Mystery of the Sand-hills

R. Austin Freeman

I have occasionally wondered how often Mystery and Romance present themselves to us ordinary men of affairs only to be passed by without recognition. More often, I suspect, than most of us imagine. The uncanny tendency of my talented friend John Thorndyke to become involved in strange, mysterious and abnormal circumstances has almost become a joke against him. But yet, on reflection, I am disposed to think that his experiences have not differed essentially from those of other men, but that his extraordinary powers of observation and rapid inference have enabled him to detect abnormal elements in what, to ordinary men, appeared to be quite commonplace occurrences. Certainly this was so in the singular Roscoff case, in which, if I had been alone, I should assuredly have seen nothing to merit more than a passing attention.

It happened that on a certain summer morning – it was the

fourteenth of August, to be exact – we were discussing this very subject as we walked across the golf links from Sandwich towards the sea. I was spending a holiday in the old town with my wife, in order that she might paint the ancient streets, and we had induced Thorndyke to come down and stay with us for a few days. This was his last morning, and we had come forth betimes to stroll across the sand-hills to Shellness.

It was a solitary place in those days. When we came off the sand-hills onto the smooth, sandy beach, there was not a soul in sight, and our own footprints were the first to mark the firm strip of sand between high-water mark and the edge of the quiet surf.

We had walked a hundred yards or so when Thorndyke stopped and looked down at the dry sand above tidemarks and then along the wet beach.

'Would that be a shrimper?' he cogitated, referring to some impressions of bare feet in the sand. 'If so, he couldn't have come from Pegwell, for the River Stour bars the way. But he came out of the sea and seems to have made straight for the sand-hills.'

'Then he probably was a shrimper,' said I, not deeply interested.

'Yet,' said Thorndyke, 'it was an odd time for a shrimper to be at work.'

'What was an odd time?' I demanded. 'When was he at work?'

'He came out of the sea at this place,' Thorndyke replied, glancing at his watch, 'at about half-past eleven last night, or from that to twelve.'

'Good Lord, Thorndyke!' I exclaimed, 'how on earth do you know that?'

'But it is obvious, Anstey,' he replied. 'It is now half-past nine, and it will be high-water at eleven, as we ascertained before we came out. Now, if you look at those footprints on the sand, you see that they stop short – or rather begin – about two-thirds of the distance from high-water mark to the edge of the surf. Since they are visible and distinct, they must have been made after last high-water. But since they do not extend to the water's edge, they must have been made when the tide was going out; and the place where they begin is the place where the edge of the surf was when the foot-prints were made. But that place is, as we see, about an hour below the high-water mark. Therefore, when the man came out of the sea, the tide had been going down for an hour, roughly. As it is high-water at eleven this morning, it was high-water at about ten-forty last night; and as the man came out of the sea about an hour after high-water, he must have come out at, or about, eleven-forty. Isn't that obvious?'

'Perfectly,' I replied, laughing. 'It is as simple as sucking eggs when you think it out. But how the deuce do you manage always to spot these obvious things at a glance? Most men would have just glanced at those footprints and passed them without a second thought.'

'That,' he replied, 'is a mere matter of habit; the habit of trying to extract the significance of simple appearances. It has become almost automatic with me.'

During our discussion we had been walking forward slowly, straying on to the edge of the sand-hills. Suddenly, in a hollow between the hills, my eye lighted upon a heap of clothes, apparently, to judge by their orderly disposal, those of a bather. Thorndyke also had observed them and we approached together and looked down on them curiously.

'Here is another problem for you,' said I. 'Find the bather. I don't see him anywhere.'

'You won't find him here,' said Thorndyke. 'These clothes have been out all night. Do you see the little spider's web on the boots with a few dewdrops still clinging to it? There has been no dew forming for a good many hours. Let us have a look at the beach.'

We strode out through the loose sand and stiff, reedy grass to the smooth beach, and here we could plainly see a line of prints of naked feet leading straight down to the sea, but ending abruptly about two-thirds of the way to the water's edge.

'This looks like your nocturnal shrimper,' said I. 'He seems to have gone into the sea here and come out at the other place. But if they are the same footprints, he must have forgotten to dress before he went home. It is a quaint affair.'

'It is a most remarkable affair,' Thorndyke agreed; 'and if the footprints are not the same it will be still more inexplicable.'

He produced from his pocket a small spring tape measure with which he carefully took the lengths of two of the most distinct footprints and the length of the stride. Then we walked back along the beach to the other set of tracks, two of which he measured in the same manner.

'Apparently they are the same,' he said, putting away his tape; 'indeed, they could hardly be otherwise. But the mystery is, what has become of the man? He couldn't have gone away without his clothes, unless he is a lunatic, which his proceedings rather suggest. There is just the possibility that he went into the sea again and was drowned. Shall we walk along towards Shellness and see if we can find any further traces?'

We walked nearly half a mile along the beach, but the smooth surface of the sand was everywhere unbroken. At length we turned to retrace our steps; and at this moment I observed two men advancing across the sand-hills. By the time we had reached the mysterious heap of garments they were quite near, and, attracted no doubt by the intentness with which we were regarding the clothes, they altered their course to see what we were looking at. As they approached, I recognised one of them as a barrister named Hallett, a neighbour of mine in the Temple, whom I had already met in the town, and we exchanged greetings.

'What is the excitement?' he asked, looking at the heap of clothes and then glancing along the deserted beach; 'and where is the owner of the togs? I don't see him anywhere.'

'That is the problem,' said I. 'He seems to have disappeared.'

'Gad!' exclaimed Hallett, 'if he has gone home without his clothes, he'll create a sensation in the town! What?'

Here the other man, who carried a set of golf clubs, stooped over the clothes with a look of keen interest.

'I believe I recognise these things, Hallett; in fact, I am sure I do. That waistcoat, for instance. You must have noticed that waistcoat. I saw you playing with the chap a couple of days ago. Tall, clean-shaven, dark fellow. Temporary member, you know. What was his name? Popoff, or something like that?'

'Roscoff,' said Hallett. 'Yes, by Jove, I believe you are right. And now I come to think of it, he mentioned to me that he sometimes came up here for a swim. He said he particularly liked a paddle by moonlight, and I told him he was a fool to run the risk of bathing in a lonely place like this, especially at night.'

'Well, that is what he seems to have done,' said Thorndyke, 'for these clothes have certainly been here all night, as you can see by that spider's web.'

'Then he has come to grief, poor beggar!' said Hallett; 'probably got carried away by the current. There is a devil of a tide here on the flood.'

He started to walk towards the beach, and the other man, dropping his clubs, followed.

'Yes,' said Hallett, 'that is what has happened. You can see his footprints plainly enough going down to the sea; but there are no tracks coming back.'

'There are some tracks of bare feet coming out of the sea farther up the beach,' said I, 'which seem to be his.'

Hallett shook his head. 'They can't be his,' he said, 'for it is obvious that he never did come back. Probably they are the tracks of some shrimper. The question is, what are we to do? Better take his things to the dormy-house and then let the police know what has happened.'

We went back and began to gather up the clothes, each of us taking one or two articles.

'You were right, Morris,' said Hallett, as he picked up the shirt. 'Here's his name, "P. Roscoff", and I see it is on the vest and the shorts, too. And I recognise the stick now – not that that matters, as the clothes are marked.'

On our way across the links to the dormy-house mutual introductions took place. Morris was a London solicitor, and both he and Hallett knew Thorndyke by name.

'The coroner will have an expert witness,' Hallett remarked as we entered the house. 'Rather a waste in a simple case like this. We had better put the things in here.'

He opened the door of a small room furnished with a good-sized table and a set of lockers, into one of which he inserted a key.

'Before we lock them up,' said Thorndyke, 'I suggest that we make and sign a list of them and of the contents of the pockets to put with them.'

'Very well,' agreed Hallett. 'You know the ropes in these cases. I'll write down the descriptions, if you will call them out.'

Thorndyke looked over the collection and first enumerated the articles: a tweed jacket and trousers, light, knitted wool waistcoat, black and yellow stripes, blue cotton shirt, net vest and shorts, marked in ink 'P. Roscoff', brown merino socks, brown shoes, tweed cap, and a walking stick – a mottled Malacca cane with a horn crooked handle. When Hallett had written down this list, Thorndyke laid the clothes on the table and began to empty the pockets, one at a time, dictating the descriptions of the articles to Hallett while Morris took them from him and laid them on a sheet of newspaper. In the jacket pockets were a handkerchief, marked 'P. R.'; a letter case containing a few stamps, one or two hotel bills and local tradesmen's receipts, and some visiting cards inscribed 'Mr Peter Roscoff, Bell Hotel, Sandwich'; a leather cigarette case, a 3B pencil fitted with a point-protector, and a fragment of what Thorndyke decided to be vine charcoal.

'That lot is not very illuminating,' remarked Morris, peering into the pockets of the letter case. 'No letter or anything indicating his permanent address. However, that isn't our concern.' He laid aside the letter case, and picking up a pocket-knife that Thorndyke had just taken from the trousers pocket, examined it curiously. 'Queer knife, that,' he remarked. 'Steel blade – mighty sharp, too – nail file and an ivory blade. Silly arrangement, it seems. A paper-knife is more convenient carried loose, and you don't want a handle to it.'

'Perhaps it was meant for a fruit-knife,' suggested Hallett, adding it to the list and glancing at a little heap of silver coins that Thorndyke had just laid down. 'I wonder,' he added, 'what has made that money turn so black. Looks as if he had been taking some medicine containing sulphur. What do you think, doctor?'

'It is quite a probable explanation,' replied Thorndyke, 'though we haven't the means of testing it. But you notice that this vesta box from the other pocket is quite bright, which is rather against your theory.'

He held out a little silver box bearing the engraved monogram 'P.R.', the burnished surface of which contrasted strongly with the dull brownish-black of the coins. Hallett looked at it with an affirmative grunt, and having entered it in his list and added a bunch of keys and a watch from the waistcoat pocket, laid down his pen.

'That's the lot, is it?' said he, rising and beginning to gather up the clothes. 'My word! Look at the sand on the table! Isn't it astonishing how saturated with sand one's clothes become after a day on the links here? When I undress at night, the bathroom floor is like the bottom of a birdcage. Shall I put the things in the locker now?'

'I think,' said Thorndyke, 'that, as I may have to give evidence, I should like to look them over before you put them away.'

Hallett grinned. 'There's going to be some expert evidence after all,' he said. 'Well, fire away, and let me know when you have finished. I am going to smoke a cigarette outside.'

With this, he and Morris sauntered out, and I thought it best to go with them, though I was a little curious as to my colleague's object in examining these derelicts. However, my curiosity was not entirely balked, for my friends went no farther than the little garden that surrounded the house, and from the place where we stood I was able to look in through the window and observe Thorndyke's proceedings.

Very methodical they were. First he laid on the table a sheet of newspaper and on this deposited the jacket, which he examined carefully all over, picking some small object off the inside near the front, and giving special attention to a thick smear of paint which I had noticed on the left cuff. Then, with his spring tape he measured the sleeves and other principal dimensions. Finally, holding the jacket upside down, he beat it gently with his stick, causing a shower of sand to fall on the paper. He then laid the jacket aside, and, taking from his pocket one or two seed envelopes (which I believe he always carried), very carefully shot the sand from the paper into one of them and wrote a few words on it – presumably the source of the sand – and similarly disposing of the small object that he had picked off the surface.

This rather odd procedure was repeated with the other garments – a fresh sheet of newspaper being used for each – and with the socks, shoes and cap. The latter he examined minutely, especially as to the inside, from which he picked out two or three small objects, which I could not see, but assumed to be hairs. Even the walking stick was inspected and measured, and the articles from the pockets scrutinised afresh, particularly the curious pocket-knife, the ivory blade of which he examined on both sides through his lens.

Hallett and Morris glanced in at him from time to time with indulgent smiles, and the former remarked:

'I like the hopeful enthusiasm of the real pukka expert, and the way he refuses to admit the existence of the ordinary and commonplace. I wonder what he has found out from those things. But here he is. Well, doctor, what's the verdict? Was it temporary insanity or misadventure?'

Thorndyke shook his head. 'The inquiry is adjourned pending the production of fresh evidence,' he replied, adding: 'I have folded the clothes up and put all the effects together in a paper parcel, excepting the stick.'

When Hallett had deposited the derelicts in the locker, he came out and looked across the links with an air of indecision.

'I suppose,' said he, 'we ought to notify the police. I'll do that. When do you think the body is likely to wash up, and where?'

'It is impossible to say,' replied Thorndyke. 'The set of the current is towards the Thames, but the body might wash up anywhere along the coast. A case is recorded of a bather drowned off Brighton whose body came up six weeks later at Walton-on-the-Naze. But that was quite exceptional. I shall send the coroner and the chief constable a note with my address, and I should think you had better do the same. And that is all that we can do, until we get the summons for the inquest, if there ever is one.'

To this we all agreed; and as the morning was now spent, we walked back together across the links to the town, where we encountered my wife returning homeward with her sketching kit. This Thorndyke and I took possession of, and having parted from Hallett and Morris opposite the Barbican, we made our way to our lodgings in quest of lunch. Naturally, the events of the morning were related to my wife and discussed by us all, but I noted that Thorndyke made no reference to his inspection of the clothes, and accordingly I said nothing about the matter before my wife; and no opportunity of opening the subject occurred until the evening, when I accompanied him to the station. Then, as we paced the platform while waiting for his train, I put my question:

'By the way, did you extract any information from those garments? I saw you going through them very thoroughly.'

'I got a suggestion from them,' he replied; 'but it is such an odd one that I hardly like to mention it. Taking the appearances at their face value, the suggestion was that the clothes were not all those of the same man. There seemed to be traces of two men, one of whom appeared to belong to this district, while the other would seem to have been associated with the eastern coast of Thanet between Ramsgate and Margate, and by preference, on the scale of probabilities, to Dumpton or Broadstairs.'

'How on earth did you arrive at the localities?' I asked.

'Principally,' he replied, 'by the peculiarities of the sand which fell from the garments and which was not the same in all of them. You see, Anstey,' he continued, 'sand is analogous to dust. Both consist of minute fragments detached from larger masses; and just as, by examining microscopically the dust of a room, you can ascertain the colour and material of the carpets, curtains, furniture coverings and other textiles, detached particles of which form the dust of that room, so, by examining sand, you can judge of the character of the cliffs, rocks and other large masses that occur in the locality, fragments of which become ground off by the surf and incorporated in the sand of the beach. Some of the sand from these clothes is very characteristic and will probably be still more so when I examine it under the microscope.'

'But,' I objected, 'isn't there a fallacy in that line of reasoning? Might not one man have worn the different garments at different times and in different places?'

'That is certainly a possibility that has to be borne in mind,' he replied. 'But here comes my train. We shall have to adjourn this discussion until you come back to the mill.'

As a matter of fact, the discussion was never resumed, for, by the time that I came back to 'the mill', the affair had faded from my mind, and the accumulations of grist monopolised my attention; and it is probable that it would have passed into complete oblivion but for the circumstance of its being revived in a very singular manner, which was as follows.

One afternoon about the middle of October my old friend, Mr Brodribb, a well-known solicitor, called to give me some verbal instructions. When we had finished our business, he said:

'I've got a client waiting outside, whom I am taking up

to introduce to Thorndyke. You'd better come along with us.'

'What is the nature of your client's case?' I asked.

'Hanged if I know,' chuckled Brodribb. 'He won't say. That's why I am taking him to our friend. I've never seen Thorndyke stumped yet, but I think this case will put the lid on him. Are you coming?'

'I am, most emphatically,' said I, 'if your client doesn't object.'

'He's not going to be asked,' said Brodribb. 'He'll think you are part of the show. Here he is.'

In my outer office we found a gentlemanly, middle-aged man to whom Brodribb introduced me, and whom he hustled down the stairs and up King's Bench Walk to Thorndyke's chambers. There we found my colleague earnestly studying a will with the aid of a watchmaker's eye-glass, and Brodribb opened the proceedings without ceremony.

'I've brought a client of mine, Mr Capes, to see you, Thorndyke. He has a little problem that he wants you to solve.'

Thorndyke bowed to the client and then asked:

'What is the nature of the problem?'

'Ah!' said Brodribb, with a mischievous twinkle, 'that's what you've got to find out. Mr Capes is a somewhat reticent gentleman.'

Thorndyke cast a quick look at the client and from him to the solicitor. It was not the first time that old Brodribb's high spirits had overflowed in the form of a 'leg-pull', though Thorndyke had no more whole-hearted admirer than the shrewd, facetious old lawyer.

Mr Capes smiled a deprecating smile. 'It isn't quite so bad as that,' he said. 'But I really can't give you much information. It isn't mine to give. I am afraid of telling someone else's secrets, if I say very much.'

'Of course you mustn't do that,' said Thorndyke. 'But I suppose you can indicate in general terms the nature of your difficulty and the kind of help you want from us.'

'I think I can,' Mr Capes replied. 'At any rate, I will try. My difficulty is that a certain person with whom I wish to communicate has disappeared in what appears to me to be a rather remarkable manner. When I last heard from him, he was staying at a certain seaside resort and he stated in his letter that he was returning on the following day to his rooms in London. A few days later, I called at his rooms and found that he had not yet returned. But his luggage, which he had sent on independently, had arrived on the day which he had mentioned. So it is evident that he must have left his seaside lodgings. But from that day to this I have had no communication from him, and he has never returned to his rooms nor written to his landlady.'

'About how long ago was this?' Thorndyke asked.

'It is just about two months since I heard from him.'

'You don't wish to give the name of the seaside resort where he was staying?'

'I think I had better not,' answered Mr Capes. 'There are circumstances – they don't concern me, but they do concern him very much – which seem to make it necessary for me to say as little as possible.'

'And there is nothing further that you can tell us?'

'I am afraid not, excepting that, if I could get into

communication with him, I could tell him of something very much to his advantage and which might prevent him from doing something which it would be much better that he should not do.'

Thorndyke cogitated profoundly while Brodribb watched him with undisguised enjoyment. Presently my colleague looked up and addressed our secretive client.

'Did you ever play the game of "Clumps", Mr Capes? It is a somewhat legal form of game in which one player asks questions of the others, who are required to answer "yes" or "no" in the proper witness-box style.'

'I know the game,' said Capes, looking a little puzzled, 'but—'

'Shall we try a round or two?' asked Thorndyke, with an unmoved countenance. 'You don't wish to make any statements, but if I ask you certain specific questions, will you answer "yes" or "no"?'

Mr Capes reflected awhile. At length he said:

'I am afraid I can't commit myself to a promise. Still, if you like to ask a question or two, I will answer them if I can.'

'Very well,' said Thorndyke, 'then, as a start, supposing I suggest that the date of the letter that you received was the thirteenth of August? What do you say? Yes or no?'

Mr Capes sat bolt upright and stared at Thorndyke open-mouthed.

'How on earth did you guess that?' he exclaimed in an astonished tone. 'It's most extraordinary! But you are right. It was dated the thirteenth.'

'Then,' said Thorndyke, 'as we have fixed the time we will

have a try at the place. What do you say if I suggest that the seaside resort was in the neighbourhood of Broadstairs?'

Mr Capes was positively thunderstruck. As he sat gazing at Thorndyke he looked like amazement personified.

'But,' he exclaimed, 'you can't be guessing! You know! You know that he was at Broadstairs. And yet, how could you? I haven't even hinted at who he is.'

'I have a certain man in my mind,' said Thorndyke, 'who may have disappeared from Broadstairs. Shall I suggest a few personal characteristics?'

Mr Capes nodded eagerly and Thorndyke continued:

'If I suggest, for instance, that he was an artist – a painter in oil' – Capes nodded again – 'that he was somewhat fastidious as to his pigments?'

'Yes,' said Capes. 'Unnecessarily so in my opinion, and I am an artist myself. What else?'

'That he worked with his palette in his right hand and held his brush with his left?'

'Yes, yes,' exclaimed Capes, half-rising from his chair; 'and what was he like?'

'By gum,' murmured Brodribb, 'we haven't stumped him after all.'

Evidently we had not, for he proceeded:

'As to his physical characteristics, I suggest that he was a shortish man – about five feet seven – rather stout, fair hair, slightly bald and wearing a rather large and ragged moustache.'

Mr Capes was astounded – and so was I, for that matter – and for some moments there was a silence, broken only by old Brodribb, who sat chuckling softly and rubbing his hands. At length Mr Capes said:

'You have described him exactly, but I needn't tell you that. What I do not understand at all is how you knew that I was referring to this particular man, seeing that I mentioned no name. By the way, sir, may I ask when you saw him last?'

'I have no reason to suppose,' replied Thorndyke, 'that I have ever seen him at all' – an answer that reduced Mr Capes to a state of stupefaction and brought our old friend Brodribb to the verge of apoplexy. 'This man,' Thorndyke continued, 'is a purely hypothetical individual whom I have described from certain traces left by him. I have reason to believe that he left Broadstairs on the fourteenth of August and I have certain opinions as to what became of him thereafter. But a few more details would be useful, and I shall continue my interrogation. Now this man sent his luggage on separately. That suggests a possible intention of breaking his journey to London. What do you say?'

'I don't know,' replied Capes, 'but I think it probable.'

'I suggest that he broke his journey for the purpose of holding an interview with some other person.'

'I cannot say,' answered Capes: 'but if he did break his journey it would probably be for that purpose.'

'And supposing that interview to have taken place, would it be likely to be an amicable interview?'

'I am afraid not. I suspect that my – er – acquaintance might have made certain proposals which would have been unacceptable, but which he might have been able to enforce. However, that is only surmise,' Capes added hastily. 'I really know nothing more than I have told you, excepting the missing man's name, and that I would rather not mention.'

'It is not material,' said Thorndyke, 'at least, not at present. If it should become essential, I will let you know.'

'M – yes' said Mr Capes. 'But you were saying that you had certain opinions as to what has become of this person.'

'Yes,' Thorndyke replied; 'speculative opinions. But they will have to be verified. If they turn out to be correct – or incorrect either – I will let you know in the course of a few days. Has Mr Brodribb your address?'

'He has; but you had better have it, too.' He produced his card, and, after an ineffectual effort to extract a statement from Thorndyke, took his departure.

*

The third act of this singular drama opened in the same setting as the first, for the following Sunday morning found my colleague and me following the path from Sandwich to the sea. But we were not alone this time. At our side marched Major Robertson, the eminent dog trainer, and behind him trotted one of his superlatively educated foxhounds.

We came out on the shore at the same point as on the former occasion, and, turning towards Shellness, walked along the smooth sand with a careful eye on the not very distinctive landmarks. At length Thorndyke halted.

'This is the place,' said he. 'I fixed it in my mind by that distant tree, which coincides with the chimney of that cottage on the marshes. The clothes lay in that hollow between the two big sand-hills.'

We advanced to the spot, but, as a hollow is useless as a landmark, Thorndyke ascended the nearest sand-hill and stuck his stick in the summit and tied his handkerchief to the handle.

'That,' said he, 'will serve as a centre which we can keep in sight, and if we describe a series of gradually widening concentric circles round it, we shall cover the whole ground completely.'

'How far do you propose to go?' asked the major.

'We must be guided by the appearance of the ground,' replied Thorndyke. 'But the circumstances suggest that if there is anything buried, it can't be very far from where the clothes were laid. And it is pretty certain to be in a hollow.'

The major nodded; and when he had attached a long leash to the dog's collar, we started, at first skirting the base of the sand-hill, and then, guided by our own footmarks in the loose sand, gradually increasing the distance from the high mound, above which Thorndyke's handkerchief fluttered in the light breeze. Thus we continued, walking slowly, keeping close to the previously made circle of footprints and watching the dog; who certainly did a vast amount of sniffing, but appeared to let his mind run unduly on the subject of rabbits.

In this way half an hour was consumed, and I was beginning to wonder whether we were going after all to draw a blank, when the dog's demeanour underwent a sudden change. At the moment we were crossing a range of high sand-hills, covered with stiff, reedy grass and stunted gorse, and before us lay a deep hollow, naked of vegetation and presenting a bare, smooth surface of the characteristic greyish-yellow sand. On the side of the hill the dog checked, and, with upraised muzzle, began to sniff the air with a curiously suspicious expression, clearly unconnected with the rabbit question. On this, the major unfastened the leash, and the dog, left to his own devices, put his nose to the ground and began rapidly to cast to and fro, zigzagging down the side of the hill and growing every moment more excited. In the same sinuous manner he proceeded across the hollow until he reached a spot near the middle; and here he came to a sudden stop and began to scratch up the sand with furious eagerness.

'It's a find, sure enough!' exclaimed the major, nearly as excited as his pupil; and, as he spoke, he ran down the hillside, followed by me and Thorndyke, who, as he reached the bottom, drew from his 'poacher's pocket' a large fern-trowel in a leather sheath. It was not a very efficient digging implement, but it threw up the loose sand faster than the scratchings of the dog.

It was easy ground to excavate. Working at the spot that the dog had located, Thorndyke had soon hollowed out a small cavity some eighteen inches deep. Into the bottom of this he thrust the pointed blade of the big trowel. Then he paused and looked round at the major and me, who were craning eagerly over the little pit.

'There is something there,' said he. 'Feel the handle of the trowel.'

I grasped the wooden handle, and, working it gently up and down, was aware of a definite but somewhat soft resistance. The major verified my observation and then Thorndyke resumed his digging, widening the pit and working with increased caution. Ten minutes' more careful excavation brought into view a recognisable shape – a shoulder and upper arm; and following the lines of this, further diggings disclosed the form of a head and shoulders plainly discernible though still shrouded in sand. Finally, with the point of the trowel and a borrowed handkerchief – mine – the adhering sand was cleared away; and then, from the bottom of the deep, funnel-shaped hole, there looked up at us, with a most weird and horrible effect, the discoloured face of a man.

In that face, the passing weeks had wrought inevitable changes, on which I need not dwell. But the features were easily recognisable, and I could see at once that the man corresponded completely with Thorndyke's description. The cheeks were full; the hair on the temples was of a pale, yellowish brown; a straggling, fair moustache covered the mouth; and, when the sand had been sufficiently cleared away, I could see a small, tonsure-like bald patch near the back of the crown. But I could see something more than this. On the left temple, just behind the eyebrow, was a ragged, shapeless wound such as might have been made by a hammer.

'That turns into certainty what we have already surmised,' said Thorndyke, gently pressing the scalp around the wound. 'It must have killed him instantly. The skull is smashed in like an eggshell. And this is undoubtedly the weapon,' he added, drawing out of the sand beside the body a big, hexagon-headed screw-bolt, 'very prudently buried with the body. And that is all that really concerns us. We can leave the police to finish the disinterment; but you notice, Anstey, that the corpse is nude with the exception of the vest and probably the pants. The shirt has disappeared. Which is exactly what we should have expected.'

Slowly, but with the feeling of something accomplished,

we took our way back to the town, having collected Thorn-dyke's stick on the way. Presently, the major left us, to look up a friend at the club house on the links. As soon as we were alone, I put in a demand for an elucidation.

'I see the general trend of your investigations,' said I, 'but I can't imagine how they yielded so much detail; as to the personal appearance of this man, for instance.'

'The evidence in this case,' he replied, 'was analogous to circumstantial evidence. It depended on the cumulative effect of a number of facts, each separately inconclusive, but all pointing to the same conclusion. Shall I run over the data in their order and in accordance with their connections?'

I gave an emphatic affirmative, and he continued:

'We begin, naturally, with the first fact, which is, of course, the most interesting and important; the fact which arrests attention, which shows that something has to be explained and possibly suggests a line of enquiry. You remember that I measured the footprints in the sand for comparison with the other footprints. Then I had the dimensions of the feet of the presumed bather. But as soon as I looked at the shoes which purported to be those of that bather, I felt a conviction that his feet would never go into them.

'Now, that was a very striking fact – if it really was a fact – and it came on top of another fact hardly less strik-ing. That bather had gone into the sea; and at a considerable distance he had unquestionably come out again. There could be no possible doubt. In foot measurements and length of stride the two sets of tracks were identical; and there were no other tracks. That man had come ashore and he had remained ashore. But yet he had not put on his clothes. He couldn't have gone away naked; but, obviously he was not there. As a criminal lawyer, you must admit that there was prima facie evidence of something very abnormal and probably criminal.

'On our way to the dormy-house, I carried the stick in the same hand as my own and noted that it was very little shorter. Therefore it was a tall man's stick. Apparently, then, the stick did not belong to the shoes, but to the man who had made the footprints. Then, when we came to the dormy-house, another striking fact presented itself. You remember that Hallett commented on the quantity of sand that fell from the clothes on to the table. I am astonished that he did not notice the very peculiar character of that sand. It was perfectly unlike the sand which would fall from his own clothes. The sand on the sand-hills is dune sand – wind-borne sand, or, as the legal term has it, aeolian sand; and it is perfectly characteristic. As it has been carried by the wind, it is necessarily fine. The grains are small; and as the action of the wind sorts them out, they are extremely uniform in size. Moreover, by being continually blown about and rubbed together, they become rounded by mutual attrition. And then dune sand is nearly pure sand, composed of grains of silica unmixed with other substances.

'Beach sand is quite different. Much of it is half-formed, freshly broken-down silica and is often very coarse; and, as I pointed out at the time, it is mixed with all sorts of foreign substances derived from masses in the neighbourhood. This particular sand was loaded with black-and-white particles, of which the white were mostly chalk, and the black particles of coal. Now there is very little chalk in the Shellness sand, as there are no cliffs quite near, and chalk rapidly disappears from sand by reason of its softness; and there is no coal.'

'Where does the coal come from?' I asked.

'Principally from the Goodwins,' he replied. 'It is derived from the cargoes of colliers whose wrecks are embedded in those sands, and from the bunkers of wrecked steamers. This coal sinks down through the seventy-odd feet of sand and at last works out at the bottom, where it drifts slowly across the floor of the sea in a north-westerly direction until some easterly gale throws it up on the Thanet shore between Ramsgate and Foreness Point. Most of it comes up at Dumpton and Broadstairs, where you may see the poor people, in the winter, gathering coal pebbles to feed their fires.

'This sand, then, almost certainly came from the Thanet coast; but the missing man, Roscoff, had been staying in Sandwich, playing golf on the sand-hills. This was another striking discrepancy, and it made me decide to examine the clothes exhaustively, garment by garment. I did so; and this is what I found.

'The jacket, trousers, socks and shoes were those of a shortish, rather stout man, as shown by measurements, and the cap was his, since it was made of the same cloth as the jacket and trousers.

'The waistcoat, shirt, underclothes and stick were those of a tall man.

'The garments, socks and shoes of the short man were charged with Thanet beach sand, and contained no dune sand, excepting the cap, which might have fallen off on the sand-hills.

'The waistcoat was saturated with dune sand and contained no beach sand, and a little dune sand was obtained from the shirt and undergarments. That is to say, that the short man's clothes contained beach sand only, while the tall man's clothes contained only dune sand.

'The short man's clothes were all unmarked; the tall man's clothes were either marked or conspicuously recognisable, as the waistcoat and also the stick.

'The garments of the short man which had been left were those that could not have been worn by a tall man without attracting instant attention and the shoes could not have been put on at all; whereas the garments of the short man which had disappeared – the waistcoat, shirt and underclothes – were those that could have been worn by a tall man without attracting attention. The obvious suggestion was that the tall man had gone off in the short man's shirt and waistcoat but otherwise in his own clothes.

'And now as to the personal characteristics of the short man. From the cap I obtained five hairs. They were all blonde, and two of them were of the peculiar, atrophic, "point of exclamation" type that grow at the margin of a bald area. Therefore he was a fair man and partially bald. On the inside of the jacket, clinging to the rough tweed, I found a single long, thin, fair moustache hair, which suggested a long, soft moustache. The edge of the left cuff was thickly marked with oil-paint – not a single smear, but an accumulation such as a painter picks up when he reaches with his brush hand across a loaded palette. The suggestion – not very conclusive – was that he was an oil-painter and left-handed. But there was strong confirmation. There was an artist's pencil – 3B – and a stump of vine charcoal such as an oil-painter might carry. The silver coins in his pocket were blackened with sulphide as they would be if a piece of artist's soft, vulcanised rubber has been in the pocket with them. And there was the pocket-knife. It contained a sharp steel pencil-blade, a charcoal file and an ivory palette-blade; and that palette-blade had been used by a left-handed man.'

'How did you arrive at that?' I asked.

'By the bevels worn at the edges,' he replied. 'An old palette-knife used by a right-handed man shows a bevel of wear on the underside of the left-hand edge and the upper side of the right-hand edge; in the case of a left-handed man the wear shows on the underside of the right-hand edge and the upper side of the left-hand edge. This being an ivory blade, showed the wear very distinctly and proved conclusively that the user was left-handed; and as an ivory palette-knife is used only by fastidiously careful painters for such pigments as the cadmiums, which might be discoloured by a steel blade, one was justified in assuming that he was somewhat fastidious as to his pigments.'

As I listened to Thorndyke's exposition I was profoundly impressed. His conclusions, which had sounded like mere speculative guesses, were, I now realised, based upon an analysis of the evidence as careful and as impartial as the summing up of a judge. And these conclusions he had drawn instantaneously from the appearances of things that had been before my eyes all the time and from which I had learned nothing.

'What do you suppose is the meaning of the affair?' I asked presently. 'What was the motive of the murder?'

'We can only guess,' he replied. 'But, interpreting Capes' hints, I should suspect that our artist friend was a blackmailer; that he had come over here to squeeze Roscoff – perhaps not for the first time – and that his victim lured him out on the sand-hills for a private talk and then took the only effective means of ridding himself of his persecutor. That is my view of the case; but, of course, it is only surmise.'

Surmise as it was, however, it turned out to be literally correct. At the inquest Capes had to tell all that he knew; which was uncommonly little, though no one was able to add to it. The murdered man, Joseph Bertrand, had fastened on Roscoff and made a regular income by blackmailing him. That much Capes knew; and he knew that the victim had been in prison and that that was the secret. But who Roscoff was and what was his real name – for Roscoff was apparently a *nom de guerre* – he had no idea. So he could not help the police. The murderer had got clear away and there was no hint as to where to look for him; and so far as I know, nothing has ever been heard of him since.

Superintendent
Wilson's Holiday

G. D. H. Cole & M. Cole

It is always a difficult job to persuade Wilson to take a holiday; for, as he is fond of saying, his work is his recreation, and he is apt to feel lost without it. On the occasion of which I am writing, however, I was adamant; for he was really badly run down after a succession of gruelling cases, and I was afraid that, unless he gave himself a rest, even his physique would give way. In my double capacity therefore, of friend and medical adviser, I brought strong pressure to bear. I not only ordered him positively to take an absolute rest, but proposed a joint walking tour, during which I made up my mind to ensure that neither cases nor adventures should come his way. Finally, as old Plato used to say, 'with great difficulty he agreed'; and that was how it was that a bright June afternoon found us walking together along the low sand-hills which border, but do not protect, the coast of Norfolk a few miles north of Yarmouth.

It was the third day of our tour. On the first we had been content with running to Norwich in my Morris-Oxford, and refreshing our memories of the old city. The next day we had poked about among the Broads, and ended up at Yarmouth, where we decided to leave the car behind and walk in a leisurely fashion right round the coast to King's Lynn, zigzagging inland to look at an old church or village as we felt inclined.

This afternoon we were walking through a region sparsely populated enough. It was a part where the sea was still steadily eating away the land, and in the memory of man whole villages had vanished. Already we had inspected the ruins of an old church, still lying strewn about the beach, where, we were told, the parson still preached one sermon yearly in order to maintain his right to the stipend. That left behind, we were walking along a very low range of sand-cliffs. One solitary house was in sight, perched on the very edge, and some miles ahead we could see the big black-and-white bulk of a lighthouse, and behind it a tall church tower.

'Upon my word, Michael,' said Wilson, 'I've got a thirst. A drink, or even a cup of tea, would come in mighty handy.' He took out the map. 'There doesn't appear to be a village nearer than that lighthouse, and that's a good three miles. There's a small place called Happisburgh just behind it, where that church tower is.'

I, too, looked at the map. 'There seem to be a few houses half a mile or so inland,' I said. 'We might get something at one of them.'

'Better push on,' said Wilson. 'There's sure to be a pub in the village. And the only house in our immediate neighbourhood doesn't look at all hospitable.' He pointed to the lonely building on the edge of the cliff ahead.

Most certainly it did not. We had come a good deal nearer while we were talking and could now see that it was no longer a house at all, but only its skeleton. More than half of it had slid right down off the edge onto the beach below; and the remainder stood desolate – roof and windows gone, with heaps of broken brickwork lying as they had fallen. The door was boarded up; but an intruder could have readily walked in through broken wall or window.

'That looks a little more promising,' I said, pointing to a bell-tent which had just come into view round the corner of the deserted house. 'If there are campers there, they will at any rate tell us the lie of the land.'

'There's quite a village of them beyond,' said Wilson. 'It looks to me like a boy scouts' camp, or something of the sort. Now's our chance, Michael, of giving one of them an opportunity for his daily good deed. The Good Samaritan up to date, you know.'

'I don't see a soul about,' I answered.

By this time, we had come abreast of the ruined cottage, and within twenty yards or so of the solitary tent. The scouts' camp, if it was so, still lay a good half mile ahead on the opposite side of a track which ran down to the beach through a gap in the cliffs. It looked very white and trim, with the sun upon it, whereas the tent nearer to us, even in the bright sunshine, still looked dirty and somehow forlorn. We passed the ruin and went towards it. Not a soul appeared.

The tent flap was waving idly about in the light wind; and, as we came up to it, we saw the remains of a fire before it, scattered broadcast by the wind, and a number of cooking utensils and other miscellaneous objects lying about.

'Slovenly people, these campers,' said Wilson. 'Apparently there's no one here; but we may as well make sure.' So saying, he strode up to the tent opening and looked in. A minute later he withdrew his head. 'You have a look too,' he said.

The inside of the tent was in wild disorder. In two places the canvas had come away from the ground, and the wind had been blowing freely through the interior. Bedclothes and a few garments were flung about here and there in confusion. Moreover, it looked as if the rain had got in; for many of the things were wet and sodden, though the tent itself appeared quite dry. There was, however, on the farther side a long tear in the canvas, and through this a shaft of sunlight was streaming in.

'Well, Michael, any deductions?' my companion asked, as I turned away.

'Only that any sensible camper would have sewn up that hole, pegged the tent down, and put out his bedclothes in the sun to dry.'

'True, O sage. And, from the fact that these campers didn't, what do you conclude?'

'It looks as if they weren't here last night.'

'Because it hasn't rained since yesterday, you mean?'

'Yes,' I answered. 'Those things must have got wet at least eighteen hours ago. No one could have slept in them in that state.'

'True,' said Wilson, 'and equally, nobody would have left them in that state if he had been here since the weather turned fine. Ergo, these campers left here before last night, and presumably in a hurry, since they didn't even stop to straighten things up, or close the tent flap. Queer campers, Michael. Now, why were they in such a devil of a hurry? It's not natural.' He stood pondering.

'Hanged if I know. Perhaps they were catching a train.'

Wilson strode round the little encampment. Suddenly, he stopped. 'Hullo!' he said. 'You see that bucket.'

'Yes; what about it?'

'Only that there isn't any water in it.'

'Why should there be?'

'My dear Michael, it rained heavily last night. A regular downpour. If that bucket had been standing there then, it wouldn't have been dry now.'

'You mean it shows they were here after it turned fine. Perhaps they went away in a hurry just after the rain stopped.'

'At midnight? To catch a train? Hardly.'

'Somebody else may have been here and put the bucket there since.'

'Perhaps,' said Wilson. He seemed to be hardly listening. Instead, he was poking about among the scattered remains of the fire. 'Eh? What's this?'

'Come off it,' I said. 'I've not brought you here to practise detecting why a pair of campers didn't wash up the dinner things. It's none of our business, thank heaven!'

'No,' said Wilson, hesitatingly, and with a faint note of interrogation in his voice. 'But this is interesting, all the same.' He held out for my inspection what looked like the charred fragment of a penny notebook.

I took it from him. 'Why,' I exclaimed, 'it's a bit of the butt-end of somebody's chequebook.'

'It is; and somebody has been kind enough to leave the number of the cheques all ready for identification.'

'I suppose a man may burn the butt-end of his chequebook if he likes.'

'But he doesn't usually burn the butt-ends of several different chequebooks over a campfire during his holidays.' Raking among the ashes, he had disinterred what were clearly the ends of two other chequebooks. In both, the numbering of the cheques was intact.

'You know, Michael,' Wilson went on, 'this is really extraordinarily odd.'

'Damn it, man, come away before you find any more mare's nests.'

Wilson chuckled. 'Mare's nests? Is this a mare's nest? That's exactly what I'm wondering, my dear fellow. It might be a singularly appropriate name. Let's have another look in here.' This time he dived right into the tent. Peering in, I saw him carefully turning over the various objects which lay strewn about it. Presently he gave a long whistle. 'Look here,' he said.

I looked. He was holding up a sheet on which, unmistakably, there was a long stain of blood. That it was blood I had no doubt. But it looked, not as if someone had bled upon the sheet, but as if some sharp, bloodstained implement had been wiped clean upon it. There were little tears in the midst of the stain, as if the sharp edge had cut into the fabric. 'What do you make of that?' Wilson asked. I told him. 'Right first time,' he observed. 'Is my medical adviser still of opinion that these campers' affairs are none of our business?'

I could no longer deny it. 'If they are,' I said, 'let me report it to the local police, while you clear out before you get involved. You've got to rest.'

'My dear Michael, I ask you. You bring me to this desolate spot, and walk me straight into the middle of a mystery. To begin with, I'm human; and secondly, this is evidently the hand of fate. Never flout Providence, Michael; she knows better even than my doctor what is good for me.'

I shrugged my shoulders helplessly. 'May it be a mare's nest,' I said, 'and may you quickly find the eggs.'

'I've just found something; but it's not an egg.' He held up his hand, and in it was a long, sharp steel blade, still unrusted.

'The weapon,' I gasped.

Wilson laughed. 'So doubting Thomas believes at last,' he said. 'Precisely – the weapon. All we require now is the corpse.'

'It doesn't follow there is a corpse,' I objected. 'Even if you strike a man with a knife, you don't always kill him.'

'A profoundly surgical observation, doctor. But we may as well see if there is a corpse all the same. At any rate, there seems to be – or to have been – a fair amount of blood about.' He went to the back of the tent and showed me on a patch of sand a large, dark stain which had soaked deeply into the ground. 'The man who lost all that blood, Michael, didn't dash off at top speed to catch a train. Let's have another look round.'

He dived into the tent, and reappeared, carrying a Norfolk

coat, a pair of grey flannel trousers and an exceedingly dirty shirt. These he proceeded carefully to examine.

'Well,' I said at last, 'what are the conclusions?'

'They are fairly obvious. The shirt is marked "H. P." Inside the pocket of the coat is a tailor's label, which announces it as the property of Alec Courage, Esq., St Mary's Mansions, SW1. It is a large coat, obviously made for a fat, but fairly short man. The trousers, on the other hand, were made for a thin man, and bear no mark. Either they belong to "H. P.", the owner of the shirt, who, by the way, may also be identifiable by his laundry mark, or they are the property of some third person unknown. We will give "H. P.", for the present, the benefit of the doubt. We have thus the traces of two men, one fat and one thin, and we have good reason for believing that we know the name of one and the initials of the other. Beyond that, there are a few obvious indications. The large man is a heavy smoker, and in the habit of carrying tobacco loose in the pocket. The small man keeps a car or motorcycle – for there are numerous petrol and grease stains on his trousers, and they are of very varying age. He has the habit of keeping his hands in his trousers pockets, and he has something wrong with his left leg. There are other inferences; but for the present they seem unimportant. It is to be observed that there are no papers of any sort in either the coat or the trousers.'

'I think I follow you so far,' I said. 'What next?'

'We will now,' said Wilson, 'look a little farther afield. And the first thing we observe strikes me as distinctly interesting. May I call your attention to the footprints, Michael?'

I looked closely at the trodden sand before the tent and

tried to follow what I knew of Wilson's methods. 'I can see signs,' I said, 'of four distinct pairs of feet – or at least I think so.'

'Good,' said Wilson.

'First, there is a large blank impression – with no nails or stud-marks or anything. Secondly, there is a rather smaller impression, in which the sole is blank, but the heel is round with a star-shaped figure in the middle. Thirdly, there is a very small pair of marks that might almost have been made by a woman. They are noticeable because of the barred impressions of the soles. And lastly, there is a pair with very large hobnails, or something of the sort. Am I right?'

'Quite right,' Wilson answered. 'And it can hardly have escaped you that pairs one and two are regularly on top of the others – or that, in fact, the large blank impression is your own crepe-rubber, while the star and the circle belong to me.' He held up his foot for my inspection.

'Oh,' I said rather ruefully. 'Then that leaves only the other two. And as we have signed our presence so plainly, and there are no other marks, it seems pretty plain that nobody except these two men has been here till we came.'

Wilson nodded. 'Yes,' he said; 'that is, since the rain, which would have washed away any previous impressions. But it also follows that these two men have been here since the rain.'

'But what about the wet camping clothes?'

'My dear Michael, that was the bucket, not the rain. Someone upset the bucket over them, and then set it upright again. And that was done since the rain, or the bucket would not have been empty. No, what we have proved is that these two men *were* here after the rain, and that they left in a hurry.'

Drawing out a piece of paper and a pencil, Wilson made a sketch. 'Let us call the small prints "A",' he said, 'and the big hobnails "B". Now, here we have "B" prints first coming towards the tent up from the road that leads inland from the beach. Then we have again "B's" prints going in the direction of that ruined cottage, and then returning. You see, he has trodden on one of his own steps just here, and that proves which way he went first. Lastly, on the opposite side, we have again "B's" prints going away inland, towards that road that comes up from the beach.' He cast about for a minute or two. 'No,' he said, 'I can find no other prints at all. "A" has left none except just in front of the tent, and "B" only some more just by the tent and these other two lines. It looks, then, as if they were both here at the same time. We have, however, tracks of "B" going away, but not of "A". Puzzle: where is "A"?'

'He's not here, at all events.'

'True. Now, suppose we try following "B's" tracks. Towards the cottage first, I think. Study the footprints carefully, and don't walk in them. They are, to say the least, suggestive.'

They suggested nothing to me, but I followed obediently. The steps led to a gap in the broken wall. Wilson, who was leading, looked in, and immediately uttered an exclamation.

In the half-room to which the gap in the wall led stood the remains of a deal table. The two walls nearest the sea had collapsed, and one leg of the table was actually standing upon air, protruding over the edge of the cliff. And on the table lay a cap, a walking stick and a mackintosh. The stick lay a little apart, and under it, as under a paperweight, was a letter. Wilson silently picked it up. It was stuck down, stamped and addressed to George Chalmers, Esq., St Mary's Mansions, SW1.

Wilson held it irresolutely in his hand for a moment. Then he produced a pocket-knife and slowly and carefully worked the blade under the flap. In a few seconds he had the letter open, leaving the envelope to all appearance intact. 'I think, in the circumstances, we will take the liberty,' he said. A minute later, he handed me the letter.

'Dear George,' it ran, 'Very sorry to leave you in the lurch, and all that. But you'll find out soon enough why I'd better not live any longer. Forgive me, if you can. Yours, Hugh.'

'Suicide!' I said. 'But how …?'

Wilson, meanwhile, was leaning over the edge of the cliff, gazing down at something below. 'Well?' I asked. 'The exhibits are complete,' he answered; 'item, one body.'

I climbed beside him and gazed down. Below us a clump of jejune bushes was growing precariously on the face of the cliff. And among them lay the body of a man, huddled up awkwardly, as it had fallen from the room in which we stood. 'I must get down to him,' I said.

It was an unpleasant scramble; but I managed it. In a minute or so, I stood beside the body. There was no doubt about the cause of death. The man's throat was slit from ear to ear. 'His throat's been cut,' I shouted up to Wilson. A minute later he stood beside me, and we gazed down together at the dead man. He was small and fair-haired, not more than thirty years old, with a face almost childishly pretty, but now frozen in a strange look of horror. And he had been dead many hours. There was no doubt of that.

Wilson spoke my thought. 'Does a suicide look like that, Michael?' he asked, gravely.

I bent down again, and studied the wound. 'This is no suicide,' I said. 'The man's been murdered.'

'Precisely,' said Wilson. 'Men do not commit suicide by first cutting their throats, and then jumping off a fifty-foot cliff into a bush. Do you mean more than that?'

'Yes, I do. That wound is not self-inflicted. The man was seized from behind, and held roughly by someone who then slit his throat … But … what does that letter mean? He said he was committing suicide.'

'Or his murderer said it for him,' Wilson answered. 'But look! What's that?'

In the bush, close by the dead man, lay an open razor, stained with blood. 'The weapon,' I said.

Wilson smiled grimly. 'You said that before,' he said. 'Two bloodstained weapons are surely an undue allowance for one throat.'

'I'm out of my depth,' said I.

Wilson by now was bending down and making a search of the body. The murdered man was dressed in a silver-grey lounge suit; and from this he quickly extracted a bundle of papers and letters. Among them were two envelopes addressed to 'Hugh Parsons, Esq.,' at an address in Hampstead. The letters and papers seemed to be purely personal, and, after a cursory examination, Wilson thrust them back into the dead man's pocket. 'Prima facie,' he said, 'this appears to be the body of Hugh Parsons, whom we can identify with the "H. P." of the shirt we found in the tent and the "Hugh" of the letter.'

'But I don't understand,' I said. 'This man has been murdered; but he has left a letter announcing his suicide. What's the explanation?'

'On the face of it, there is one obvious answer. Parsons has been murdered, and his murderer has tried to make it look like suicide.'

'But the letter?'

'If we are right, then the letter is a forgery. We can't tell for certain, at present; but I think we may safely accept the hypothesis of murder. To begin with – we found sufficient reason to suspect a murderous attempt *before* we had even encountered the body or the suggestion of suicide.'

'As a suggested suicide,' I observed, 'it doesn't seem very successful. It didn't deceive you at all.'

'Nor could it have deceived anyone for five minutes,' Wilson said. 'Let's go over the points. First, we have a plain set of footprints leading to and from the cliff. They are not the dead man's. Secondly, there are no footprints of the dead man leading here, though he clearly came, or was brought, here after the rain; for his body is quite dry, though the ground under him is still damp. Thirdly, we have the traces up at the tent simply shouting "Murder". And, fourthly, we have two bloodstained weapons instead of one. No murderer could possibly have thought this arrangement made a plausible suicide. Yet he left it like that. Why?'

'Perhaps he staged the suicide, and then was surprised before he had time to remove either his own footprints or the traces up at the tent.'

'That is possible; but I don't think it is correct. For we know he wasn't actually surprised. There are no other footprints. Of course, he might have got panic and done a bunk. But he didn't. The steps leading inland from the tent are those of a man walking slowly.'

'Then what is the explanation?'

'Part of it, I think, is clear. The murder was done just by the tent. Then the murderer carried the body here and staged this absurd suicide. If you remember the tracks, "B's" stride was shorter, and the impressions of his feet were much deeper when he was coming this way than on his return. That suggests that he was carrying a heavy burden – to wit, the body. What I don't understand is why he didn't clear the traces away. As he left things, he was bound to be seen through. And then, again, you say the wound was obviously not self-inflicted.'

'He may not have had medical knowledge enough to know that,' I said.

'He must have had enough to know that two weapons were not likely,' Wilson said. 'And that just deepens the mystery. The thing's so well done in some respects, and so badly in others. Now, why?'

'I'm damned if I know,' said I. 'Do you?'

'I can think of at any rate one possible explanation,' Wilson said, puckering his brow. 'But I'm not at all sure that it will work. Anyway, our immediate job, I suppose, is to tell the local police what we've found.'

It was not, however, quite our next job. For at this moment a voice – a fresh, young voice – hailed us from above. 'Hullo!' it said. 'Something wrong here. Bill!' Looking up, we saw two boy scouts staring down at us as we stood beside the body.

'Something very much wrong,' said Wilson. 'Do either of you boys know this man?'

With extraordinary agility, the two boys clambered down beside us. 'It's one of the blokes from that tent up there,' he said.

'There were two of them, weren't there?' Wilson enquired.

'Three. Leastways, two of them was campin' out 'ere, and there was a friend of theirs stayin' at the Bear and Cross.'

'Where's that?'

''Bout a mile inland, up the track. 'E 'ad a car wiv 'im, and used to drive it down 'ere.'

'When did you last see any of them?'

'Mr Chalmers – 'e's the chap with the car – ain't seen him for two or three days. But I seen the other two night before last. Quarrellin', they was. Oo! D'yer think t'other chap done this one in?'

'Somebody's done him in,' said Wilson. 'Now, mind, nothing up here or at the tent must be touched till the police come. But I've a job for you chaps. I want you to hunt all down this bit of cliff and see if you can find anything that might throw more light on this affair. And, Michael, I've a job for you too. I'm going to stay here till help comes. But I want you to buzz off and find the nearest telephone, and get straight on to the police station at Norwich. Tell them I'm here, and they're to send an inspector and some men out in a car at once. See? And then go to the Bear and Cross, and see if this Mr Chalmers is still about, or what's become of him. And find out anything you can about those two fellows down at the tent. When that's done, come back here, and, if you value your life, don't forget to bring a couple of bottles of beer and some sandwiches.'

By the time we had clambered up to the ruined cottage, several more boy scouts had appeared on the scene. Wilson at once took command, and set them to hunt the entire neighbourhood for clues. One was assigned to me as guide to the Bear and Cross, where, it appeared, the nearest telephone was to be found. As I left the scene of the crime, I saw Wilson neatly covering the tell-tale footsteps with a blanket taken from the tent.

At the Bear and Cross, I found no difficulty in carrying out Wilson's suggestions. In the presence of a gaping landlord, to whom I had given the barest minimum of information, I rang up the police station at Norwich, and was lucky enough to get through at once. A recital of the main facts sufficed to secure a promise that an inspector should be despatched at once to the scene of the crime, and, as soon as I mentioned Wilson's name, there was no mistaking the alacrity with which the local police took up the case. But I did not want to waste time; and as soon as I could, I rang off, and turned my attention to the landlord.

He seemed a typical country innkeeper enough – an ex-soldier by the look of him, and indeed I soon found he had been a sergeant in a regular regiment before the war and had seen plenty of service in France. His great desire was to question me; but I speedily made it plain that I meant to get more information than I gave, and before long I had him talking.

The two campers in the tent – Hugh Parsons and Alec Courage – had been there for about ten days, and had had their letters sent to the inn. The previous weekend, a friend of theirs, named George Chalmers, had come down with his car, and had put up at the inn. He had stayed only a few days, and had returned to town on Tuesday, leaving the other two behind. The two campers had been before his coming regular visitors at the inn; and during the weekend they had been there more than ever, and Chalmers had several times taken them out in his car – a Morris-Oxford. Three days ago, on Tuesday afternoon, Chalmers had received a telegram, and on receipt of it had announced that he must go back to town at once. The other two had been with him when it came, and they had stayed to take a farewell drink together and to see him off. The last the landlord had seen of them was their going off arm in arm, and a little unsteadily (for it had been a wet leave-taking) along the track towards the sea. He had been rather surprised to see nothing of them for the past three days; for previously they had been frequent and thirsty visitors at the inn. But it was quite possible that, now their friend was no longer there, they had transferred their attention to the Swan at Happisburgh. It was only a couple of miles or so from their camp.

At my suggestion the landlord rang up the Swan, and found that his surmise was correct. The two men had spent the greater part of Wednesday there, drinking and playing billiards and strumming on the piano – for the day had been wet. They had also walked over together on Thursday afternoon, and stayed for a drink and a game. The Swan, however, had seen nothing of them since then, and it was now late on Friday afternoon. There were, I ascertained, no other licensed premises within several miles. This seemed to bear out the conclusion already formed that the murder had taken place some time on Thursday night.

'What sort of man was Courage?' I asked. The landlord's view was that he was a bit of a sport – an athlete, too, by his talk; shortish, but very strongly and sturdily built, with curly dark hair and a small moustache – about thirty years of age.

'We found a queer-looking long knife down at the tent,' I said; 'a very thin, sharp blade about eight inches long, with a white bone handle. Do you know it?'

'Why,' said the landlord, staring. 'I shouldn't wonder if it was my ham and beef knife. I lost it on Tuesday after those chaps were here. You don't mean it was—'

'It may have been the weapon,' I said. 'Anyway, it's at the tent now. One of them must have picked it up. Could they have got at it easily?'

'It was kept in a drawer in the parlour, where they were all sitting. And, now you mention it, I remember Mr Courage went back in there after Mr Chalmers had driven off. He may have taken it then.'

'When did you see it last?'

'When I put it back in the drawer after lunch on Tuesday. When I wanted it on Wednesday morning it wasn't there.'

'Any of them could have taken it?'

'It must 'a' been Mr Courage, when he went back into the parlour.'

That was the sum of the information I gleaned; but, as I made my way back to the scene of the tragedy, accompanied

by the boy scout bearing a plentiful supply of Bass and sandwiches, I felt well enough pleased with it. It all seemed to fit
in; and especially the theft of the knife from the inn seemed
to prove that the crime had been premeditated for at least
two days before its actual execution. Parsons was dead, and
Courage was presumably his murderer. Else why had the
man vanished off the face of the earth? Courage, too, was
proved to have had ample opportunity for stealing the knife.
Things certainly looked black for Mr Alec Courage.

I found Wilson the centre of an excited group of boy
scouts, among whom was a man, dressed as a scoutmaster,
whom I had not seen before. Wilson hailed me cheerily, and,
seizing a bottle of Bass from my companion, took a long pull.
'That's better,' he said.

I told my news, which seemed to please him, while he hun-
grily ate a sandwich. 'We've some news too,' he said, 'and it's
rather curious. To begin with, Mr Evanson here knows a bit
about our two friends.'

The scoutmaster proceeded to explain. He and Courage
had been at school together; but they had not met for years
until their accidental encounter a few days before. Indeed,
Mr Evanson gave it clearly to be understood that, in his view,
Courage was a good deal of a bad hat. Meeting, however, by
chance on the beach, they had renewed their old acquaintance and exchanged experiences. Courage had introduced
Parsons to him, and explained that they were partners in a
firm of outside brokers in the City. Evanson had gathered
that their business was highly speculative; indeed, they had
spoken of it in the spirit of gamblers who enjoyed playing
for high stakes. He had met Chalmers once at the Bear and

Cross, and gathered that he was the senior partner in the concern.

On the tragedy itself Evanson could throw no direct light. He said he had last spoken with the two friends on Thursday afternoon, when they were going down to the sea for a bathe. They had told him of Chalmers' return to town, and had announced that they were staying on at least for another week. They had seemed in the best of spirits and on excellent terms with each other.

That was the end of Evanson's direct evidence. But he produced one of his boys, who had been in the neighbourhood of the tent later on Thursday evening. The boy said that he had heard high voices, as of two men quarrelling, proceeding from the tent, and had caught some words about 'a tight place' and 'letting a pal down'. The boy had not thought much of it at the time, and had, in fact, forgotten all about it till the discovery of the tragedy brought the incident back to his mind.

Evanson's story seemed to me quite straightforward. He gave of Courage a most unflattering portrait, which showed that he thought him quite the sort of man who might be guilty of a serious crime. Of Parsons he seemed to know little, but to regard him as in all probability a harmless 'pigeon' who had fallen into Courage's skilful hands. But I, at any rate, was disposed to discount a good deal of Mr Evanson's testimony; for it was obvious that he was more than a bit of a prig.

'Come over here, Michael,' said Wilson; 'there's something I want to look at again.'

'Anything fresh since I went away?' I asked, as soon as we were alone.

'Yes and no,' was the answer. 'You know those footprints of "B" leading inland from the tent?' I nodded. 'Well, there's an odd thing about them. You remember I said that Mr "B's" stride was shorter and his footmarks deeper on the way to the ruined cottage than back?' Again I nodded acquiescence. 'Well, those steps leading inland from the tent are the same as those leading to the cottage – short and deep.'

'I don't quite see what you mean,' I said.

'I concluded from the first lot of footsteps that "B" had been carrying a heavy burden going to the cottage, but not on his return. That squared with our finding the body on the cliffs below the cottage. But how does it square with our finding the same sort of footsteps – deep, and close together – leading from the tent in the opposite direction?'

'It doesn't seem to square at all,' I said. 'Where do the other footsteps lead, by the way?'

'They go to the road leading to the inn; and there they stop. The road surface is too hard to leave an impression.'

'Then you simply don't know where "B" went after he reached the road?'

'That's where those boy scouts come in. I set them to search, and one of them says he's found some of "B's" footsteps again a bit farther up the road, leading off into a disused path that apparently runs along parallel to the cliffs. I've had no chance to follow it yet; but the boy says the tracks are quite plain. Hullo, that must be the police!'

A car was running swiftly down the road that led from the Bear and Cross to the sea. In it were two policemen and a man in plain clothes. Wilson went to meet the car, and it came to a stop about a hundred yards from the tent. I hung in the background while the plainclothesman deferentially saluted Wilson. They remained a minute or two in conversation, and then came over towards me. 'This is Inspector Davey,' said Wilson. 'My friend, Dr Prendergast.'

In a few minutes Wilson had given the local inspector a full account of what we had so far discovered. 'We'll leave you to look round here,' he said then, 'while we follow up these footsteps.' But we were not destined to follow them just yet; for, as we turned to leave the inspector, a second car appeared, coming at full speed along the road from the Bear and Cross. 'Hullo, who's this?' said the inspector.

The second car – a new Morris Oxford – came to a stop beside the police car, and its sole occupant, a tall, broad man of forty or so, came hastily towards us. 'What the devil's all this?' he said. 'My name's Chalmers. They told me up at the pub there was something wrong.'

The inspector glanced at Wilson. 'You are Mr George Chalmers,' said the latter.

'Yes. Is it true that Parsons is dead?' The big man seemed greatly agitated.

'He was a friend of yours?' Wilson asked.

'My partner – he and Mr Courage, who was staying here with him. I've just run down from town to see them, and they told me at the inn ...'

'What did they tell you?'

'That Parsons was dead, and Courage had disappeared. Is that true? What has happened?'

'Mr Parsons left this letter for you, Mr Chalmers,' said Wilson, handing over the note which we had found at the ruined cottage. 'We took the liberty of opening it.'

Chalmers took the note, and read it with puckered brows. 'I don't understand,' he said. 'The landlord said Parsons had been murdered. But this means suicide. Though why—'

'You do not know of any reason why Mr Parsons should have taken his life?'

'The thing's preposterous. Now, if it had been Courage, I might have understood. This is the devil of a business. I say, I suppose anything I tell you won't go any further – I mean, unless it has to, you know.'

'I think,' said Wilson, 'you had better tell us frankly all you know, Mr Chalmers.'

'It's a beastly business,' said Chalmers, 'and I don't understand it at all. You realise, Parsons and Courage were my partners – we're stockbrokers, you know. Ten days ago, the two of them came away here on a holiday together, leaving me to run the show in town while they were away. Last Friday, my bank manager asked me to come round and see him. I went, and he produced a cheque, drawn to bearer for a very large sum on the firm's account, and asked me if it was all right. It was signed with Courage's name and mine. I told him at once the damned thing was a forgery and I'd never signed any such cheque. It was a damned good forgery, mind you; and I could hardly tell the signature from my own. Well, to cut a long story short, we went into the accounts, and we found that during the past week several other bearer cheques had been paid out, all purporting to be signed by Courage and me – and all forgeries, so far as my signature was concerned at any rate. Of course, I was in the devil of a stew – I may tell you the cheques were big enough to cause our firm serious embarrassment. We rang up the police at once and put the matter in their hands, and then I went back to the office, collected the chequebooks in which the counterfoils were, and buzzed off down here with them to see Courage. Of course, I assumed his signature had been forged as well as mine.

'Well, over the weekend, we had a tremendous confab about it. Courage said he'd never signed the cheques, and couldn't give any explanation. But we knew the chequebooks had been locked up in a safe to which only we three had the keys. Finally, Courage and Parsons fell out about it, and accused each other of forging the cheques. I trusted them both, and told them it was all nonsense, and at length they made it up and shook hands. I stayed down here till Tuesday, keeping in telephonic communication with London all the time. Then, on Tuesday, I got a wire from the office, asking me to go up to town at once over some important business. And now comes the beastly part of the affair. I had to go to Courage's desk for some papers this morning, and there I found, in his blotting book, some unmistakable transfers of a series of attempts at my signature. Of course, that put the lid on it. I simply buzzed down here at once; and I don't mind telling you I meant to cut my losses and advise Courage to make himself scarce. We've been close friends, and I'd sooner lose all I have than have to put him in the dock over it. You can say that's compounding a felony if you like. Anyway, it's what I meant to do. I got to the Bear and Cross a few minutes ago, and there the landlord told me Parsons was dead and Courage vanished. Of course, I was dumbfounded. Forgery's one thing; but murder's another. I came right on here to tell you all I know. But, of course, if it's suicide ... though why on earth ...' His voice tailed away.

'It was not suicide, Mr Chalmers,' said Wilson. 'It was murder. The suicide was merely a clumsy pretence. The murderer burned, or endeavoured to burn, the butt-ends of the chequebooks, and then made off.' And in a few words he told Chalmers the state of the affair.

Chalmers seemed more and more downcast. 'I'd never have believed it,' he said at the close.

'Well, what's your conclusion now?' Wilson asked.

'I've no wish to draw conclusions. Unfortunately, they seem too obvious.'

'You mean that Courage killed Parsons and fled. But why should he kill Parsons?'

'I suppose Parsons must have found out that he had forged the cheques. He killed him in order to shut his mouth, and then got panic and ran away.'

'Parsons, you think, was entirely innocent?'

'Lord bless you, yes. Hugh Parsons had nothing to do with this. No, it was Courage who forged the cheques, sorry as I am to say it.'

'Well, Mr Chalmers, will you kindly go with the inspector here and identify Parsons, and give him any help you can?' Wilson drew the inspector aside and communed with him a moment. 'Now, Michael,' he said. '*A nos moutons.*' We waited until Inspector Davey and Chalmers had disappeared into the ruined cottage, and then set off up the road. 'About here is where the boy found the footprints,' said Wilson. 'Yes, here they are. He's a sharp lad.'

The footprints were rather faint; but there was no doubt that they had been made by the same boots as the 'B' prints by the tent. There were only two or three of them visible, for the track was loose sand, and so overgrown that the rain had only penetrated at one or two points. But it was quite clear that they were leading away from the tent along a sunken lane which ran parallel to the shore and about a hundred yards from it, and was screened from view by a thick covering of bushes on either side. We walked along the track for a little distance. I could see no further marks; but Wilson's more experienced eyes seemed to be satisfied that he was still on the trail. Eventually, after about five minutes' walking, the lane came out on a wider track leading on one side up to the main road inland, and on the other still keeping roughly parallel to the shore.

'Hullo!' said Wilson. 'There's been a car here. You notice the tracks. And just here it stood for some time. You can see the oil ran down and made a little pool. Dunlop tyres, with a noticeable patch on the left back wheel. That may come in useful. The tracks run both ways – up to the road, and in the other direction – a double track each way. Left turn, I think.' He led the way along the track, away from the main road.

For some distance we followed the track, which, though wider here, was still sunken. Marks were few and far between; but Wilson seemed sure that we were still following the trail of the car. After about a mile the track bent round in the direction of the shore, and within five minutes brought us out, through another gap in the low cliffs, right on the beach, and within a few yards of the ruined church we had already visited earlier in the day. No tyre marks were visible on the beach; either the wind had obliterated them all from the loose sand, or, if the car had descended below high-water mark, the tide had been up and washed them away.

But Wilson strode unhesitatingly towards the ruin, which stood well above high-water mark, temporarily protected by a range of low artificial sand-hills planted with juniper. There he paused and stared meditatively at the bushes.

'What on earth do you expect to find here?' I asked.

'Who knows,' he returned. 'One can but look.'

'But for what?'

'For what one may find. Look here, for instance.' I looked, but could see nothing but the sandy soil between the ruins. 'Trampled ground,' Wilson interpreted. 'And recently trampled. But someone's obliterated all clear marks. Anyway, we might as well experiment there as anywhere. Prod with your stick.' So saying, he began prodding with his own, thrusting it in as deep as it would go into the sand at one place after another. I followed his example. In some places the stick, with a little coaxing, went right down. In others, it was speedily stopped by something hard below the surface. 'Never mind the hard stuff,' said Wilson. 'That's masonry from the church. Try for something soft but resistant.' A minute or so later he gave an exclamation. 'This feels like something, Michael,' he said. 'Come and help me clear away the sand.'

With sticks and hands we cleared away the loose sand as best we could. Less than a foot down, my hand caught hold of something hard but yielding. Together we scraped for a moment and brought to light a human boot. Another followed, and within a few minutes we had exposed to view the entire body of a man, buried a foot deep below the drifting sand. He was a young man, short but stout and strongly built, with a crisp black moustache, and to all appearances not long dead. And the manner of death was evident. Round his neck a cord had been tightly knotted, and the stained and swollen flesh plainly showed the marks.

I had been too occupied first in scraping away the sand and then in making a brief inspection of the body to give vent to my curiosity till now. But when I had assured myself how the man had died, I turned to Wilson. 'What in God's name does this mean?' I cried. 'Was this what you were looking for?'

'Permit me to introduce you to the suspected murderer, Mr Courage,' he said.

'Courage!' I exclaimed. 'Then who ...' But a sharp exclamation from Wilson cut short my sentence. He had turned the body over, and now from beneath it he drew a big gold cigar case, which gleamed brightly in the evening sun. He pressed the catch and the case flew open. Within were two fat cigars, and with them a scrap of paper – a tearing from a newspaper. Wilson read it and passed it to me. It was an extract from the city page of the *Financial Times*, describing the dramatic slump in the shares of the Anglo-Asiatic Corporation.

'From yesterday's paper,' said Wilson. '*Yesterday*'s, mark you.'

'Why not?' I asked.

'The *Financial Times* is hardly likely to be on sale at Happisburgh,' he answered. 'This grave was made last night, or at all events the man died then. How did a bit of yesterday's *Financial Times* get into his grave?'

'It may have come by post,' I hazarded.

'We can probably find out whether he received any

204

newspapers by post. The question is whether this is his cigar case or someone else's. If it's someone else's, we're in luck.'

'But how did it get into the grave?'

'Do you ever dig, Michael? If you do, and don't take precautions to secure your loose property, as likely as not you'll drop some of it, and cover it over before you find out your loss. If the murderer has been kind enough to drop his cigar case for us, I say we're in luck. And I'm inclined to think he has. Judging from Mr Courage's coat which we inspected at the tent, he was a pipe, and not a cigar smoker.'

'But how do you know this is Courage?'

For answer, Wilson bent down and felt in the dead man's pockets. They were entirely empty. 'I don't,' he said at last. 'But I'll bet you anything you like it is. You see, I've been looking for him.'

'You suspected – this?' I asked.

'Certainly. It was plain from the first that we were meant to see through the pretence of suicide – plain that the murderer had meant us to see through it. But, once we did see through it, all the surface indications pointed to Courage as the murderer. Clearly that would not do. If Courage had been the murderer, either he would not have wanted us to see through the suicide, or he would have arranged that, when we did see through it, the clues should not point to him. Ergo, Courage was not the murderer. Then where was Courage, and why had he disappeared? One possible explanation was that he had taken fright and run away, even though he was innocent of the murder. But a far more plausible theory was that he had been murdered too.

'That theory was confirmed by a study of the footprints.

205

We concluded, on good evidence, that the murderer had been carrying a heavy burden on his way from the tent to the ruined cottage. We found we were right. He had been carrying Parsons. But we had equally good evidence that he was carrying a burden in the second set of footprints leading to the car; for they too were deep, and showed a shortened stride. The inference was clear. The murderer had also been carrying a body towards the car. But that body could not be Parsons. Who was it? Obviously Courage himself.'

I listened to this convincing deduction with increasing amazement. At this point I broke in. 'But his boots, man! Look at his boots!' For the boots on the feet of the body before us were identical with the 'B' tracks we had found at the tent.

'I have looked at his boots,' said Wilson. 'That is the final link in the argument. We found three sets of "B" footprints, did we not? One set led up from the shore to the tent, a second from the tent to the ruined cottage and back again, and the third from the tent to the path we have just followed.' I nodded. 'Very well,' said Wilson. 'Now observe that the left boot on the body has two nails missing. If you go back to the tent, you'll find that of our "B" footprints, set number one has those two nails missing; sets number two and three have not. This man's boots have two nails missing. Otherwise, the tracks are the same. Now, do you see?'

'You never told me that,' I said reproachfully.

'You looked at them just as much as I did,' said the provoking fellow. 'Can you now tell me what they mean?'

'Mr "B" was two men,' I said, rather sulkily. 'And only one of them is Courage.'

'Precisely. Two men with almost identical boots – but

fortunately not quite identical. Does that suggest anything to you?'

'Only a very odd coincidence, I'm afraid. And, of course, the fact that we have to look for a new murderer.'

'Yes,' said Wilson. 'Perhaps we'd better start.'

Wilson left me to watch by the body while he went back to the tent to inform the police and summon assistance. But hardly had he left me when the scoutmaster, Evanson, appeared, scrambling down the cliff by a narrow path. I did not quite know what to do; for Wilson had said that he was particularly anxious, for the present, to keep the finding of the second body a secret. But I did not see how I could keep the newcomer away. I went towards him in the hope of heading him off.

'What were you two doing here?' he asked. 'I happened to notice you from the path above and I thought I'd come down and see if you had found anything fresh. Have you?'

'I'm afraid,' I said, 'I'm hardly at liberty ...'

Evanson shook his head. 'No, I'm going a bit farther along the pry. But, while I am here, I want to have a look at these ruins. Any objection?'

'Well,' I said, 'if you don't mind ...'

At this moment his hat, lifted by a gust of wind, went flying along the beach. He followed it, and, with some dismay, I watched the chase end within a few feet of the shallow hole in which the body lay. I ran after him.

'My God! What's this?' I heard him say. 'Courage!'

I came up, panting, 'Well, Mr Evanson, since you have seen this, I must ask you not to say a word about it to anybody. It is most important that no one should—'

'But Courage! I thought Courage was the murderer.'

'If he was, Nemesis has soon overtaken him.'

'How did you find him? Who——?'

I was scarcely able to answer; for suddenly, on the firm sand, I had noticed the print of the scoutmaster's feet. They were, to say the least, extraordinarily like the 'B' footprints we had seen at the tent, and tracked to the lonely grave in the sand. And they were a perfect impression, without a nail missing. 'We tracked him here,' I said.

Evanson clearly noticed something odd in my manner, for he looked at me strangely. I did my best not to show my excitement; and I flattered myself that, after my first start of astonishment, I managed pretty well. Evanson went on plying me with questions, direct and indirect; and I did my best to make answers that sounded innocent, and at the same time gave nothing away. The man was not to know I suspected him if I could help it. But it was wearing work; and I was mightily relieved when the police car came running down the track and the local inspector leapt out beside us.

'Thank you, doctor, for keeping watch for us. I see Mr Evanson is here. Does he recognise the body?'

'It is Courage,' said Evanson. 'But I thought ...'

'Lord bless you, sir, we all thought. In a case like this, one's apt to think a lot of the wrong things before thinking of the right one. And now, you won't mind leaving me to manage this little affair myself. The superintendent says he would like to see you at the inn, doctor.'

I had been hesitating whether or not to tell the inspector of my discovery. But it seemed best to keep it for Wilson's ear. 'Are you coming back towards the tent?' I asked the scoutmaster.

Evanson shook his head. 'No, I'm going a bit farther along the shore,' he answered. I wondered if Wilson would blame me for letting him go; but on the whole that seemed preferable to giving my knowledge away. I left him, and set off at a smart pace towards the inn.

There, the sound of voices attracted me to the sitting room. I found Wilson there with George Chalmers. Eagerly I asked Wilson to let me speak to him for a moment alone. He came out at once, and I told him what I had found, and expressed my fear that Evanson might even now be making his escape. To my chagrin, I found that my news was no news to him. 'Yes,' he said, 'I noticed Evanson's boots when we were talking to him by the ruined cottage. But I don't think he'll run away, all the same.' He smiled.

'Not now he knows the other body has been found?'

'I think we'll chance it,' said Wilson, leaving me to wonder whether he had really something up his sleeve, or whether in this case he was not quite up to the mark. Sadly disappointed, and more than a little perplexed, I followed him back into the room where Chalmers was still sitting.

'I've just been getting Mr Chalmers to give me all the particulars about this man Courage,' he said. 'For purposes of offering a reward for his apprehension, you know.' I took the hint. Chalmers was to know nothing yet of the discovery of Courage's body.

'Now, Mr Chalmers,' Wilson went on. 'You say Courage and Parsons quarrelled badly over the weekend, but had made it up before you left.'

'Yes.'

'Since you went away, have you either heard from, or communicated with, either of them?'

'No.'

'Is there any way you can think of in which either could have got to know what you have since discovered about Courage?'

'Impossible. I only found it out myself this morning.'

'But it is possible Mr Parsons may have found out somehow for himself?'

'Yes, that's possible. But I don't see how.'

'Then how do you explain what happened?'

'I don't like having to explain it at all. But I fear the facts speak for themselves.'

At this point Wilson's tone suddenly changed. 'Was your firm in Anglo-Asiatics, Mr Chalmers?' he said sharply.

Chalmers gave a violent start, and seemed unable to make up his mind what to answer. 'I don't see what bearing—' he began.

'I only asked,' said Wilson sweetly, 'because I noticed you cut out that bit about it from Wednesday's *Financial Times*.'

'What the devil d'you mean?'

'Well, you did, didn't you?'

'Certainly not,' Chalmers snapped.

'You see,' said Wilson, 'I thought you had, because we found the cutting in your cigar case. This is yours, isn't it?' He passed the heavy gold case across the table.

Chalmers stared down at it as if the opulent little object were a snake. 'Yes,' he said, 'that's mine. I must have left it behind here on Tuesday.'

'Oh, no, I think not, Mr Chalmers. The landlord here saw you take it out, and light a cigar just as you started the car. And he is sure you put it back in your pocket.'

'He's mistaken. I must have left it behind at the tent, or it couldn't have been found there.'

'It wasn't found at the tent, Mr Chalmers. It was found on the sands beside the old ruined church at Eccles. Does that refresh your memory?'

This time there was no mistaking Chalmers' consternation. His hand shook so violently that he knocked the cigar case to the floor with a clatter.

'What! Oh, I – I walked that way on Tuesday. I must have dropped it then.'

'With a cutting from Wednesday's *Financial Times* inside?'

'Somebody must have found the case, and put the cutting in, and dropped it later.'

'It was not dropped. It was buried.'

'I – can only say I have not had it since last Tuesday.'

Wilson changed the subject. 'On Tuesday, you drove back to London in your car?'

'Yes.'

'Where has the car been since then?'

'In my garage, except when I was using it in town.'

'It has not been out of your possession?'

'N – no.'

'Then, if your car was down here yesterday, we can take it that you were here too. Is that so?'

'It was not here yesterday. I was in London all day.'

'Supposing I tell you that you and your car were seen to

turn off the main road and stop at a point where two tracks join on the way between here and Eccles, and that subsequently your car was driven down to a point near the church at Eccles, and near where the cigar case was found?'

Chalmers' alarm seemed to increase with every word that Wilson spoke. 'It's not true,' he said wildly. 'I tell you I've been here since Tuesday.'

'Are you aware that your car has a highly distinctive patch on the left back tyre, Mr Chalmers?'

Chalmers had apparently made up his mind by now what to say. 'Look here,' he said, 'this is a ridiculous misunderstanding. You're quite right. I did drive that way. But it was on Tuesday.'

'Come, come, Mr Chalmers. The marks could not possibly have survived the rain. Will you tell me where you were on Thursday, if you were not here?'

Chalmers sprang up. 'That's enough,' he said furiously. 'I thought third-degree methods were confined to the American police. I tell you I have not been near the place since Tuesday last, when I left Parsons and Courage alive and well!'

'And what makes you think Mr Courage is not alive now?' Wilson asked sharply. Chalmers saw his slip and made a sudden movement for the door. Opening it, he stepped straight into the arms of a large Norfolk policeman.

'George Chalmers,' said Wilson, signing to the policeman, 'I arrest you for the murder of Hugh Parsons and Alec Courage. And I warn you that anything you say may be used in evidence against you.'

A minute later, when the policeman, assisted by another, had led Chalmers away, I turned to Wilson.

'But what about Evanson's boots?' I cried.

'My dear Michael, what about them? They had the same arrangement of nails – it's a common one – but they were at least a size and a half too small.'

'Then it was I after all who discovered the mare's nest.'

'I'm afraid it was, Michael,' said Wilson gently. 'We all do at times.'

'I'll get my own back on you when you have that nervous breakdown,' said I. But Wilson only laughed.

Of course, Wilson's work did not end with the arrest of Chalmers. We might be as morally certain as we liked that he had murdered both his partners, but proof was another matter. Wilson himself admitted that it was Chalmers' own suspicious manner at the interview just described which had decided him to risk an immediate arrest, rather than give the man the chance of destroying incriminating evidence. And it was as well that he did so; for in Chalmers' rooms at the flat which he shared with Courage in St Mary's Mansions were found not only the copy of the *Financial Times* from which the incriminating cutting had been torn, but also a pair of boots, the twin of those on the dead man's feet, except that they had all their nails intact. They were half a size smaller than Chalmers' own footgear, and were still partly covered with Norfolk sand. Thirdly, in the desk, at the back, there turned up a scrap of paper covered with attempts at Courage's signature.

Armed with this last piece of evidence, Wilson interviewed the bank, with the result that the forged bearer cheques were submitted to further expert examination; and it was discovered that, of the two signatures which they bore – those of Courage and Chalmers – the former was really the forgery, though it had been executed so cleverly that no suspicion of it had been entertained by the bank. Chalmers had deliberately so written his own signature that it would be easily recognised as a forgery, whereas he had been at pains to make the imitation of his partner's signature as plausible as possible. This conclusion was borne out by a piece of paper found where it had blown behind the desk in his study. On this he had actually tried out both signatures. This discovery led to a close investigation of Chalmers' affairs, from which it eventually transpired that, having got the firm into serious difficulties through unwarrantable speculation, Chalmers had converted the sums represented by these cheques into bearer securities, which he had retained in preparation for the inevitable collapse.

At this point Courage's solicitor, who had also been his personal friend, disclosed a statement made by the dead man just before leaving for his holiday. In this Courage explained that he had detected a certain amount of irregularity and had eventually connected it with Chalmers. Receiving no satisfactory explanation from the latter, he had taken with him to Norfolk certain of the papers and chequebooks of the firm, with the object of discussing the position fully with Parsons, and deciding on a line of action. (These were the chequebooks whose butt-ends we found at the tent, Chalmers having burnt just enough of them to create additional suspicion and bolster up his own story.)

Even with this evidence the Crown had a hard struggle to get its conviction. Chalmers and his lawyers fought to the very last gasp, blackened Courage's character – which, indeed, was none of the best – and poured scorn on the story reconstructed by Wilson; namely, that Chalmers, having failed to secure his partners' complicity in his frauds, had decided to murder them both, and then, knowing that suspicion would almost certainly be directed to himself, had staged the clumsy pretence of suicide, which was, of course, intended to lead straight to Courage as the murderer. Even supposing the police did not see through the pretence, Courage's disappearance, together with Chalmers' statements about the forged cheques, would have amply sufficed to throw suspicion on him, and prevent any search for another criminal. What finally clinched the case against Chalmers was, curiously enough, his own alibi for the fatal night, which he had prepared with care and which very nearly saved him. Eventually, however, the police proved it to be a palpable fraud; the defence collapsed, and Chalmers was hanged.

'The Happisburgh murderer,' Wilson said to me one day when the case was over, 'illustrates one important point in the science of crime. Chalmers had brains. No one could have planned murder much better than he planned it; but he was a clumsy executant. At every point, he lacked technique. Thus, he failed to make the suicide plausible enough. It was so barefaced a fake that it was obviously meant to be seen through. But, if that was so, one naturally distrusted the obvious explanation of the murder to which it pointed when one saw through it. Then again, he dropped his cigar case, and he failed to obliterate the traces of his car. If he had merely carried Courage's body a short distance and buried it in the sand, and then really carefully obliterated the traces, I very much doubt if we should ever have found it, and then the odds are he would have got off scot-free. No, Michael, a really good criminal needs two things – brains and technique. Chalmers had plenty of brains; but, as an executant, the fellow was a bungler. The combination of brains and technique is fortunately rare – or we policemen should never catch our hares. Which would be a great pity.'

I agreed. It was wonderful how well Wilson was looking. Our little holiday in Norfolk had quite set him up.

Man Overboard

Edmund Crispin

'Blackmailers?' Detective Inspector Humbleby finished his coffee and began groping in his pocket for a cheroot.

'Well, yes, one does of course come across them from time to time. And although you may be surprised to hear this, in my experience they're generally rather nicer than any other kind of crook.

'Writers of fiction get very heated and indignant about blackmail. Yet, by and large, it's always seemed to me personally to be one of the least odious and most socially useful of crimes. To be a blackmailer's victim you do almost invariably have to be *guilty* of something or other. I mean that, unlike coshing and larceny and embezzlement and so forth, blackmail has a – a punitive function—

'Naturally, I'm not claiming that it ought to be encouraged.' Having at last disinterred his cheroot, Humbleby proceeded to light it. 'At the Yard, we have plenty of occasions for thinking that we're being deprived of evidence against a suspect in order that someone else may use it for private profit.

'On the other hand, a blackmailer can *acquire* such evidence more easily than we can – not having Judges' Rules to hamper him – and like Socrates in the syllogism, he's mortal. The death of a known blackmailer is a great event for us, I can tell you. It's astonishing the number of "Unsolved" files that can be tidied up by a quick run through the deceased's papers. Sometimes even murders – Saul Colonna, for instance; we'd never have hanged him if a blackmailer hadn't ferreted out an incriminating letter and then got himself run over by a bus.'

'Two Armagnacs, please,' Gervase Fen said to the club waiter. 'Colonna? The name's vaguely familiar, but I can't remember any details.'

'It was interesting,' said Humbleby, 'because the incriminating letter didn't on the surface *look* incriminating at all … There were these two brothers, you see, Americans, Saul and Harry Colonna. They came over here – their first visit to England – early in April of 1951, Saul to work in the office of the London correspondent of a Chicago paper, Harry to write a novel.

'New country – fresh beginning. But they'd hardly had a chance to unpack before Harry succumbed at long last to the cumulative effects of his daily bottle of bourbon. With the result that *his* first few weeks among the Limeys were spent at a sanatorium in South Wales – Carmarthenshire, to be exact: no alcohol, no tobacco, lots of milk to drink, regular brisk walks in the surrounding countryside – you know the sort of thing.

'Harry didn't like that very much. His brisk walks tended to be in the direction of pubs. But at the same time he did acquire an awe, amounting almost to positive fear, of the formidable old doctor who ran the place. So that when at last he decided that he couldn't stand the regime any longer, he felt constrained to arrange for a rather more than ordinarily unobtrusive departure, such as wouldn't involve him in having to face a lot of reproaches for his failure to stay the course. Quite simply, abandoning his belongings, he went out for one of his walks and failed to return.

'That was on the afternoon of 7 May. About midday next day, *both* brothers arrived by car at Brixham in Devon, where they took rooms at the Bolton Hotel; for after only a month's journalism Saul had been sacked, and so had been free to respond to Harry's SOS from the sanatorium, and to assist in his flight. Once in Brixham, they proceeded to enjoy themselves. Among other things, they bought, actually *bought*, a small Bermudan sloop. And did quite a lot of sailing in it …

'Then, on the evening of the 12th, having ignored numerous warnings from the weather-wise, they got themselves swept out into mid-Channel by a gale. And in the turmoil of wind and darkness Harry was knocked overboard by the boom and drowned.

'That, at least, was Saul's account of the matter, when the Dartmouth lifeboat picked him up; and it was a credible story enough. Even the subsequent discovery that Harry's life had been well insured, and that Saul was the beneficiary, failed to shake it. If a crime *had* been committed, it was undetectable, the police found – with the inevitable result that in due course the insurance companies had to pay up. As to the body, what was left of that came up in a trawl about the beginning of September, near Start Point. By then there wasn't much chance of diagnosing the cause of death. But the teeth identified it as Harry Colonna beyond any reasonable doubt ...

'So that without Laking, that would have been the end of that.

'Barney Laking was clever. He was a professional, of course. Though he'd been inside several times, he always went straight back to blackmail as soon as he'd done his term ... So you can imagine that when a number 88 ran over him, in Whitehall, we lost no time at all getting to his house. And that was where, among a lot of other very interesting stuff, we found the letter – *the* letter.

'To start with, we couldn't make anything of it at all. Even after we'd linked the "Harry" of the signature with Harry Colonna, it was still a long while before we could make out what Barney had wanted with the thing. However, we did see the light eventually ... Wait and I'll do you a copy.'

And Humbleby produced a notebook and began to write. 'I looked at that letter so hard and so often,' he murmured, 'that it's engraved on my heart ...'

'Envelope with it?' Fen asked.

'No, no envelope. Incidentally, for the record, our hand-writing people were unanimous that Harry Colonna *had* written it – that it wasn't a forgery, I mean – and also that nothing in it had subsequently been added or erased or altered ... There.'

And Humbleby tore the sheet out and handed it to Fen, who read:

You-Know-Where,
6.5.51
Dear Saul,
I'm just about fed with this dump: time I moved. When you get this, drop everything and bring the car to a little place five or six miles from here called Llanegwad (County Carmarthen). There's a beer-house called the Rose, where I risked a small drink this morning: from 6 on I'll be in it: Private Bar (so-called). Seriously, if I don't move around a bit I'll go nuts. This is URGENT.
Harry.

'M'm,' said Fen. 'Yes. I notice one thing.'

'Actually, there are two things to notice.'

'Are there? All right. But finish the story first.'

'The rest's short if not sweet,' said Humbleby. 'We had Saul along and confronted him with the letter, and of course he said exactly what you'd expect – that this was the SOS Harry had sent him from the sanatorium, properly dated and with the distance from Llanegwad correct and so on and so forth. So then we arrested him.'

'For murder?'

'Not to start with, no. Just for conspiracy to defraud the insurance companies.'

'I see … Part of it is simple, of course,' said Fen, who was still examining Humbleby's scrawl. 'When an American uses "6.5.51" in writing to another American, he means not the 6th of May but the 5th of June … On the other hand, Saul and Harry, having settled in England, may have decided that it would save confusion if they used the English system of dating all the time.'

'Which is just what Saul – when we pointed the problem out to him – told us they had decided to do.' Humbleby shook his head sadly. 'Not that it helped the poor chap.'

Fen considered the letter again. And then suddenly he chuckled.

'Don't tell me,' he said, 'that 6 May 1951, was a *Sunday*?'

'Bull's eye. It was. Sunday in Wales. No pubs open for Harry to have even the smallest of small drinks at. Therefore, Harry was using the American system of dating, and his letter was written on 5 June, four weeks after he was supposed to have been swept overboard into the Channel. Insurance fraud.'

'And Harry getting restive in his hideout near the sanatorium, and Saul suddenly thinking how nice it would be not to have to share the insurance money …'

'So back to Brixham, unobtrusively, by night, and out to sea again in the sloop. And that time,' Humbleby concluded, 'Harry really did go overboard.'

'And you have found enough evidence for a murder charge?'

'As soon as we stopped worrying about 12 May, and started concentrating on the period after 5 June, we most certainly did. Mind you, it *could* have been difficult. But luckily Saul had had the cabin of the sloop revarnished at the end of May, and we found human blood on top of the new varnish – not much, after all that time, but enough to establish that it belonged to Harry's rather unusual group and sub-groups. Taken with the other things, that convinced the jury all right. And they hanged him ...

'But you see now why I'm sometimes inclined to say a kind word for people like Barney Laking. Because really, you know, the credit in the Colonna case was all his.

'Even if I'd possessed that letter at the outset, I could quite easily have missed its significance. I only worked hard on it because it had come from Barney's collection, and I knew he didn't accumulate other people's correspondence just for fun.

'But *he* had no such inducement, bless him. With him it was just a consummate natural talent for smelling out even the most – the most deodorised of rats. What a detective the man would have made ... Do you know, they gave me a full month's leave at the end of that case, as a reward for handling it so brilliantly? And it was all thanks to Barney ...'

And Humbleby reached for his glass. 'No, Gervase, I don't care what novelists say. I like blackmailers. Salt of the earth. Here's to them.'

Credits

'Weight and See' by Cyril Hare is reprinted by permission of United Agents on behalf of the Cyril Hare Estate

'Error at Daybreak' by John Dickson Carr is reprinted by permission of David Higham Associates on behalf of John Dickson Carr

'Razor Edge' by Anthony Berkeley is reprinted by permission of The Society of Authors as the Literary Representative of The Estate of Anthony Berkeley

'Daisy Bell' by Gladys Mitchell is reprinted by permission of David Higham Associates on behalf of Gladys Mitchell

'The Furies' by Michael Innes is reprinted by permission of Peters, Fraser and Dunlop (www.petersfraserdunlop.com) on behalf of Rights Limited

'Man Overboard' by Edmund Crispin is reprinted by permission of Peters, Fraser and Dunlop (www.petersfraserdunlop.com) on behalf of Rights Limited

While every effort has been made to contact copyright-holders of each story, the editor and publishers would be grateful for information where they have been unable to trace them, and would be glad to make amendments in further editions.